𝔖𝔞𝔤𝔞

THE LAST NORSE OF WEST GREENLAND

A. S. LYONS

SAGA: THE LAST NORSE OF WEST GREENLAND

A. S. LYONS

BIC Classification:
FV (Historical Fiction), FT(Sagas).

978-0-9942525-5-5

contents

1327

Freda plucked at the talisman round her neck that was given to her by her dead mother, as she walked along the bleak shoreline of west Greenland. Her husband Orm carried their one year old son Halfdan. He grinned and crackled with laughter. His board chest jarred and strands of blonde hair fell over his blue eyes as he asked;

"Is that one of your mother's things from Vinland? No one can go there anymore, the sea is just too wild," he ridiculed, with his nose screwed up as he swung his head back and forth.

"Oh yes—mother would never admit to being a Skraeling from here in Greenland. No, she had to be from the Abenaki tribe in Vinland. Taken captive by a ship's crew bringing back timber. My father saved her soul when he married her and gave her a secure life. But the stories she told...little Halfdan might like them, they are quiet funny, unlike the saga of the Viking Orm the Bold." laughed youthful Freda while her black hair and olive skin were caressed by the wind.

Vinland summoned up an image of a perilous voyage, to a land brimming with people who had sent their Viking ancestors running for their long ships, except for Orm the Bold. His ancestors had successfully engaged in trade with violent Skraelings without losing a man, but alas he was the one and only man to achieve the monumental feat. Never to be repeated. The conversation collapsed along with thoughts of Vinland. Orm's line of vision was suddenly vexed by a blurry apparition.

Orm's pupils dilated for a moment, but he rejected the spectacle as just a figment of his imagination. He rubbed his eyes and looked again; there was a white square sail above a wooden vessel which was sailing down the Lysu Fiord.

"A ship flying...the royal standard! They haven't forgotten us! This is marvelous Freda. Think of it - trade again. And the east settlement folk won't be able to cheat us this time. We must hurry and get back to the farm." Orm's voice raced with excitement.

Ten year old Thorfinn ran along the stony shoreline to join Orm and Freda.

"Have you seen the Royal ship approaching Thorfinn?" asked Orm stretching out the palms of his hands with a mouth opened so wide it wasn't able to stretch any further.

"Yes my father and his men have gone to the church," replied Thorfinn completely lacking in excitement and strolling off.

A stifled squeak escaped Orm's throat. Thorfinn's father and his men were ardent followers of the Norse Gods, so why had they gone to a church? It couldn't be from fear of the Royal ship, that wouldn't instill any fear in those men. He could hardly wait to relate this baffling odd occurrence to his father. That joke would have to go on hold though, the Royal ship's visit held priority.

"Orm forget the ship for now. Look over there - Grimar!" Freda, sick with horror, pointed fanatically down the shoreline, to where adolescent Grimar was hooting and howling chasing after a five year old Skraeling child.

The child fell, screaming in terror. Orm sped to the child's aid without a thought, for neither Orm nor Freda were shackled with Inuit hate.

"I am going to skin you, Skraeling!" sang Grimar with a whistling hoot.

Before Orm reacted, ten year old Thorfinn saw the child under attack and charged down the shoreline, leaping on to Grimar's back and hurling him to the ground. Grimar clamored to his feet, dark revenge invading his mind. With an open mouth and exposed teeth he snarled at Thorfinn.

"One day you and yours will pay, Thorfinn!" cursed Grimar, pushing back his long brown hair.

Thorfinn stood aside with his hands defiantly on his hips and gave a snort of disgusted laughter. Thorfinn's creed demanded the he be brave, loyal, and in all things do his share.

Orm stomped up to Grimar and grabbed hold of his hair.

"Get yourself back to the farm. My father gave you a home. No one else would because you are called Grimar the fool, because think you are going to be living at the King's court one day. Well you have been caught! In an act of madness! Your harming that child could have resulted in the settlement being attacked by the Skraeling. My father will be warming your backside, later," promised Orm with vigor.

Grimar broke free and chaotic malice rejected reason, he shouted obscenities in a rattling voice busting with venom. His short legs thumping the ground, he ran off in the direction of the wharf that sat by Lysu fiord with Sandnes farm resting nearby.

The little Inuit boy rose to his feet.

"I am Fresh Water one day I will repay you," promised the boy in a tiny frightened voice.

None of them could understand the boy but his gratitude needed no translation.

Orm raised his arm and pointed to an Inuit camp in the distance. The boy ran off to join his people.

"I have to get back to Sandnes farm Thorfinn, my father is headman in the west settlement and will want us to honour the king's men."

"My father thinks they are coming to collect men for another miserable runt of a crusade to get back the unholy land," giggled Thorfinn as he brushed back his blonde hair.

A crusade; the concept picked away much of Orm's jubilation for the royal visit. Kings had indulged in that futile occupation for over two centuries. Lives and wealth lost and not a mile of holy land won back.

Freda caught up with her young husband.

"Orm your father will be expecting you to be with him," promoted Freda.

"Yes we had better hurry," replied Orm cheerfully. He dismissed Grimar and Thorfinn from his thoughts as he and Freda strolled back along the shoreline.

The wharf near Sandnes farm was a hive of activity. The headman had trimmed his beard and hair, put on his best attire made from seal skin, with a polar bear fur collar. An ancient sword was at his side.

Stalking like an assassin at the back of the assembled bodies, was Ingrid the Wise, a devout follower of the Norse Gods. She was noted across the settlement for her insight and medicine. She gave her services freely to Christians and Pagans, and was well loved by all. Ingrid carried her one year old daughter Astrid, who was going to be dedicated to Thor.

Untamed freedom lived in the hearts of West Greenlanders, and terrible demons with no idea of freedom were arriving on the ship, to have supper at people's tables, in Ingrid's judgment. The state of exuberance among the people sadly told her that any warning she might give would drown away, eclipsed by the joy of expected trade. Ingrid fled the scene in order to warn her husband of the fever sweeping the settlement in the trivial hope of trade.

The head-man calculated the nails, axes, and timber the settlement desperately needed. These commodities were absolutely essential. The settlement had to have at least two ships. The weather that had once been so kind was fading with very passing winter. Their very survival could depend on having ships to escape Greenland. The winters may yet return to normal but in the event the weather deteriorating further, the people had to be able to move, which meant having ships. There only ship was lost last summer. Its battered shell floated up the fiord, the crew and timber cargo all lost.

Driftwood and nails made of wood didn't make stout ships. Just a fishing vessel fit only to row round the fiords. The king's official must be made to understand the settlements urgent need for ship building equipment. The settlement had ivory and furs to trade.

Orm and Freda joined him at the edge of the wharf.

"The King and church have not forgotten us and many would have us believe this, just because a church was burnt in 1294 due to the church's tithe," proclaimed the headman to the hundred odd people present at the gathering beside the wharf.

They had come from miles around to see this glorious sight. Eyes were transfixed on the fiord; every minute seemed like an hour.

"I wonder what news they will bring of the outside world?" uttered Freda, riddled with excitement and hungry for news.

"I and the men want to know how much we will get paid for our furs and ivory, woman! We need nails and many other things. Orm has a list ready for them. After all we lost nine men hunting for those things, we can't let our produce go cheap", the headman replied, fully determined to get decent nail axes and timber for their goods. He didn't appreciated his daughter in- law's input into men's affairs.

The men nodded in firm agreement, they wanted goods in exchange for the furs and ropes.

"Let us welcome them first before discussing trade," suggested kindly Freda.

"We will do that," assured the headman with a determination to focus on trade.

Grimar watched with hateful eyes from the slope near the wharf. Hunting and fishing needn't fill his needs. He had to convince the captain of that ship to take him on as crew, to escape the wrath of the headman and the constant jeers from other boys, calling him Grimar the Fool. He had to concoct a delicious tale ripe for the ears of the ship's captain. Fear mingled in Grimar as he witnessed the headman shouting; soon he would shout at him and beat him again. Grimar worried about how he could escape from the Settlement. That ship drawing into the wharf was his only ticket out.

"Rest easy men, I will get as much as I can. Now let us greet them in true Norse fashion," assured the headman.

The people were gathered at the edge of the wharf to welcome the King's ship. The very moment the ship drew near to the wharf the crowd released a deafening cheer, arms waving in the air.

The King's official tax collector was very pleased with the jubilant welcome.

"The 1294 riot has obviously been forgotten. These people are faithful subjects of the King and of Mother church. Even if they do look like savages," remarked the tax collector who viewed the people as lowly peasants from the ship's deck.

The black robed priest at his side drew in a questioning breath.

"Ah my son that could be a trick to make us think they are poor. Their attire could be designed to show poverty," the priest advised skeptically.

"I hadn't thought of that. Perhaps I am being too trusting of these people. After all we haven't stepped ashore yet. It is good that you're here to advise me. I'm only twenty and have never carried out a mission such this," the young tax collector replied, making a mental note not to pay undue attention to people clothes, as it could be a disguise.

"The church too has heard of grumblings. Let us wait and see if these people are faithful to King and Church before we judge them, my son."

"Yay...yay!" cheers and shouts echoed off the lofty cliffs. Young boys ached to hear stories from Norway and Iceland, locking their vision on to the single white square sail. The tension was passionate by the time the ship moored at the wharf.

The headman and six men walked in procession to welcome their valued guests. All the men had spent an hour grooming their beards and hair to look good for this auspicious occasion.

The subject of their delight strutted from the ship, finely attired in red with gold trimmings, with his hair and beard done immaculately. Rapturous cheers broke out with each step he took. The tax collector wallowed in the admiration being heaped on him.

The priest's words fell away.

"Welcome good master," declared the headman loudly and jovially.

"Hmmn—I see that over half of the settlement must he here," said the tax collector. This pleased him—he wouldn't have to sail past every horrid farm in Greenland, and could make a swift departure from this ugly outpost of the King's domain. The man pondered on whether this one was worth keeping. It was expensive to send a ship this far out.

"The women have hot cooked seal meat for you and your men," offered the headman.

Seal meat caused the tax collector's taste buds to revolt at the very thought of that meat touching them. Mutton venison, fine cheeses, and cherries were what his palate was accustomed to.

"The men will be delighted," replied the tax collector giving them the unpleasant task of eating the Greenland food. They were after all lowly sailors and could stomach anything. The tax collector had already decided the amount of revenue he had to collect, plus there was the cost of the voyage, which had to be paid for by the people of the Settlement. He then had to collect twenty percent for taxes, and the church also wanted ten percent.

"You must want to rest after such a long voyage," remarked the headman.

The tax collector gazed at the stone house with turfs roofs, the animal's skin and fur attire on the headman. The fiords of the West Settlement were a place he wished to leave with all due haste. It was time to find out if these people really were faithful to King and Church.

"Time for that later. I will begin to collect the King's taxes and the Church tithe," declared the tax collector with a radiant smile.

His words paralyzed the welcoming party. The King and Church had sent a ship across miles of open sea, just to steal from the r long suffering people of the West Settlement. Not to trade furs for nails and woods, but simply to take what little they had. Rebellion surged in people's hearts. Black anger contorted the men's faces.

"Taxes and tithe! We are poor! We want goods in exchange for our furs and ivory not to give you goods! Be gone with you robber! Be gone!" yelled the headman his hand ripping his sword from its scabbard and sweeping it through the air. The swishing sound terrified the tax collector, and he took a step back in fear.

Enraged men vented their anger, astonishing the tax collector. The people had expected to receive goods for trade. He was a tax collector not a trader. A Royal ship didn't trade with far-flung domains in Greenland. These people had to conduct their own trade. The King was desperate for money. The Church too had many demands on its income.

These rebellious subjects had not the slightest desire to pay dues to the King or the Church. He had never heard of such disgraceful conduct. The priest had been wise to warn him. He was surrounded by rebels. These people were not subjects, but rebels. They had no wish to pay any tax or church tithe. Not one coin had been offered. In fact the rebels wanted paying! The King wanted to be paid. The Church also had the right to payment; but the rebels didn't want to pay them either. It was an affront to God as well as to the King. Christianity demanded obedience and order. Norway hadn't comprehended such rebellion existed in the West Settlement of Greenland. This Settlement was not faithful to the Church or loyal to the King. The rebels thought only about themselves—not the Church, not even their king—just themselves.

"Go! Go!" was the chanting cry of the people on the wharf, waving their fists and raising swords. One boy threw a stone and missed.

"Pity boy, try again and get the robber. He is a raider and he would rob his own people!" shouted one man waving a spear at the side of the crowd.

Armed men on the ship pointed arrows at the settlers. Women almost wept at the sight, they had spent the morning cooking and preparing to welcome these men into their homes, and they were nothing more than wolves, waiting to devour anything they had. Their arrows were like the polar bear's teeth.

"To think we had welcomed them," sobbed one pregnant woman.

"So this is what we can expect from the Church and King—theft and war," declared the headman in fury as he cursed his naive assumption and good faith. But he made a vow, for the sake of his people and his honour, to make amends.

The tax collector walked back trembling until he reached the safety of the ship. The King and Church would have to seize its payments by force. The people of this West Settlement were the most unfaithful souls the king and church had. The King and the Bishop would hear of their outrageous behaviour the moment the ship docked in Norway. The King and church was going to be paid, even if every soul in the West settlement had to die, at the point of an arrow or sword. Defiance like this could not be tolerated. The priest rushed to support the tax collector.

"I had no idea, they are rebels. Out right rebels!" The tax collector complained, seating himself on a barrel, shaking his head. He was still unable to believe what had occurred.

"I was attacked. Attacked! But pay they will. I will have the King's taxes and the Church's dues. What horrid people..." wailed the tax collector. His trust was shattered.

The people on the wharf could hardly believe the Norse customs were dead. The ship came to steal furs and ivory that was hard won, at the cost of lives.

Freda cursed herself for her folly. Trade—they hadn't come to offer anything for their goods, nothing at all. People throughout the Settlement had waited and prepared a warm welcome for bunch of pirates.

"Taxes and tithe," hollered one woman, whose husband had died on a hunting party.

The headman released a growl of anger. "Send out boats and warn our neighbors that the King and Church are coming to take what little they have, and tell them to hide their goods!" snarled the headman to the crowd that encircled him.

Angry shouts ripped though Ingrid's ears when she reached the top of the hill. Ingrid followed Grimar's route, Ingrid stopping to glare at him.

"Ah—Grimar the Fool, why don't you tell the men on that ship that you are a poor suffering Christian orphan, seeking to live at the King's court." Ingrid's mocking laughter grated Grimar's nerves, as she hurried past him on the narrow dirt path.

Waves of loathing and lust for revenge crippled Grimar's capacity to think. Then he gazed at the ship. The witch may have had a decent idea. If he told the men on that ship that he was a unwelcome Christian orphan living on pagan land, he might gain passage out of the Settlement. Grimar strolled down to the barren beach. To his great joy, six men climbed out of a boat to meet him.

"Be careful. The men at the next farm are armed and waiting to attack you, good masters," cautioned Grimar in the most concerned tone he could muster and a frightened expression to match.

The five sailors wrinkled their noses at Grimar, for they saw him as a traitor and a coward, trying to get revenge for some minor injury to his person. The priest however noted the cross round Grimar's neck.

"The boy is a Christian!" exclaimed the black robed priest in fluttering delight.

The man's tone indicated to Grimar he had just passed his first test in the art of deceit. The silly bit of ivory round his neck had done the trick, plus his sweet words had gained him attention.

"You must have good Christian parents," praised the priest as he inspected Grimar.

Grimar remembered Ingrid's words and was secretly amused that the witch was going to help him out of Greenland.

"I am an orphan and have to go from one house to another. No one wants a child here who doesn't follow Thor. I am a Christian." Grimar tried make his voice sound distressed and hoped the men couldn't pick up on his false statement. The priest's jaw dropped and he stared at Grimar in horror. An accusation of heresy had been made. The boy looked too young and innocent to know the implications of such tidings. The child was an orphan and unwanted; therefore it was his Christian duty to take him. With a touch of kindness the boy might reveal more about the West Settlement. He had been suspicious before about the strength of Christian faith in the Settlement, and now this. He would write a report for the Bishop. Bad vibes gripped him, he felt the devil walked and watched on this land.

"How would you like to come with us, what is your name?"

"Grimar. I would like that every much, good master."

"I am a priest, you will call me Father."

"A real priest...", gasped Grimar, feigning awe and respect.

Ingrid had caught up with Thorfinn, and they broke into laughter at the sight of Grimar climbing into the boat with the black robed priest.

"Grimar is in the boat?" queried Thorfinn.

"It looks as if Loki's envoy has got his passage out of Greenland. I doubt he will like the work he will be doing though. A boy without family influence! And unlettered! Gaining a position at the King's court? I think not. The church might take him, but I know he couldn't stick to their regime. Lowly hard work and ridicule will be his reward," uttered Ingrid, then she noticed the boat was heading towards her farm.

"They are heading for your farm, I will run and get the men!" yelled Thorfinn. He sprinted away instantly as he sensed imminent danger.

Ingrid sped over rough terrain to her one room stone wall house with turf roof. Men were at her door when she arrived.

"We demand tithe and taxes, woman and now!" growled the tax collector glaring at Ingrid.

"I have nothing to give. I need the furs to keep me and my Astrid warm in the cold winter months ahead," she said sharply and hurried into her house.

The priest and tax collector were indignant. A lowly woman had refused outright to pay taxes and tithe to the King and Church and in a rude manner. She had no respect for King or Church. Punishment had to be administered, otherwise the rest of the heathens in this Settlement would be taking lessons from her. They rushed after Ingrid and slammed the door behind them.

"You should be thinking of your soul. Not comfort for your child. It's soul too could be endangered by your actions!" lectured the priest furiously. "This woman hasn't even attempted to find one tenth of her belongings to offer to her church."

"My child comes first, you fiends!" yelled Ingrid.

The tax collector raised his arm to strike Ingrid, just as her husband came though the door. He grabbed the tax collector's arm and flung him over his shoulder. The tax collector ripped his sword from his side and waved it at Bjarni.

"A thin bit of ice like you, wants to—take me?" laughed Bjarni, he picked up his shield and twirled the shield round, hitting the tax collector's forearm with the shield. The sword fell to the ground. The tax collector immobilized in horror, heard Bjarni laughing.

The tax collector's assistant snuck up from behind and plunged the axe into Bjarni.

Ingrid heard the crunch that split her husband's skull. His body went stiff for a moment. His mouth opened but no sound escaped. His dying body hurtled to the floor.

More men poured into the house to support the tax collector.

"Bjarni!" she screamed and fell to her knees, holding her husband's brain as it had spilled from his cranium. Blood spewed out as he lay on the floor at Ingrid's feet.

"Take the furs off the beds; they will pay for their sins. His soul is doomed. And you are excommunicated!" exclaimed the outraged priest.

The priest marched out of the house. Ingrid rocked back and forth, holding her husband's head and wailing loudly in grief.

Ingrid was still wailing with grief, when Thorfinn's father and men pushed open the door.

"Ingrid what has happened?" asked Thorfinn's father. The men were aghast at the sight of Bjarni with his head split open on the floor.

"The Church and the King came to take what furs I had. When I told them I had none to give the man went to strike me. Bjarni came home and saw it and attacked the man, and they killed him with an axe," Ingrid was still sitting on the floor holding her husband's head and weeping.

"A man may defend his wife and must!" snarled one man, who was follower of Thor.

"Christian rabble, they came to rob and now they come to kill!" Thorfinn father's concluded Norse customs had ruptured in Norway.

The men's rage grew into a fever. They hungered for the blood of the murderers and began to weave plans on how to kill them slowly.

"Anyone at home?" asked a youthful voice from outside.

"Come in Orm," said Thorfinn's father roughly, in no mood to be polite.

Orm's breath paused the second his eyes rested on the hideous sight of Ingrid on the ground with seven angry men looking down at her husband's dead body.

"The Church and King killed him. They attacked Ingrid because she didn't want them to have her furs," explained Thorfinn's father.

Orm was repulsed but pulled himself together. A woman with a young child needed him to be a man, not a feeble weakling.

"We must get her to my boat and back to Sandnes, to the women folk. She needs them now," said Orm firmly though still in shock at such a display of brutality. It was against Norse customs. A Norse community had to act as one, when times were hard. Norway's morals had deteriorated. Iceland, he knew, still held firm to Norse customs. Norway had clearly abandoned them.

Thorfinn's father and Orm supported Ingrid out of the house and down the sloping ground to Orm's boat. Orm and Thorfinn's father rowed her to Sandnes farm.

The men of the Itivifik Fiord zoomed round the rocks, and to their heart felt joy and delight, found that the would-be victim hadn't left. In fact the vile haughty creature was roaming along a pasture, outside Ingrid's house.

Thorfinn's father had a lasso with him and hurled it round the assistant tax collector's neck. Choking heavily he was unable to cry out for help as he was hauled along the ground. Only when he was near the rocks did he finally think to use the sword at his side to cut himself free.

Thorfinn's father jumped on the blade.

"Thanks—that is a fine blade. Too good for you," mocked Thorfinn's father.

The tax collector's assistant kicked furiously as the men tried up his feet and hands.

"Wait. There is polar bear wandering the shoreline, why not give it some dinner? No one will blame us or the Skraeling then," suggested one man.

"What good idea. Can't let you die in battle. That is too honorable for you," agreed Thorfinn's father, grinning malevolently. Horror filled the assistant tax collector. He tried to scream for help, but the noose was too tight. Strong arms lifted him on to their shoulders.

"Better tempt the bear a bit," Thorfinn's father said, slicing open the victim's leg, and letting the blood ooze out. Then the men tossed the victim down the slope to the waiting bear. With the noose no longer round him, he let out a wild scream for help.

The huge white bear launched itself onto its hind legs. The bear's claws dug into the man's body and ripped him into two. His screams rode on the air and into the ears of men from the royal ship, further up the shoreline. They sped with weapons in hand to answer the call.

Part of the victim's body was being carried away by the bear when the armed men arrived at the shoreline.

"Look at the size of thing, he didn't stand a chance," one man remarked.

***

The next day Ingrid stood out overlooking the fiord.

"Oh great Thor, I have served you since childhood as my mother did before me. Sink the ships that came to steal and kill. Raise up your hammer and strike the sea!" Ingrid placed her child on the ground.

"Thor, this child I dedicate to you. Give her health and happiness in a warm land." Ingrid's chilling voice was as cold and forbidding as the ice floe in the fiord.

Ingrid watched a ray of sunlight fall on her baby daughter and knew her prayers had been an answered. Her daughter Astrid had been accepted by Thor.

"Oh Astrid, Thor has accepted you. Mighty Thor will take you from this land to walk in sunlight during winter. Just wait my little Astrid, you will leave this land, only a descendant of Einar of the Orkneys, who has a true Viking warrior will be worthy of you. He must be brave loyal and above other men."

The tax collector and the priest turned up at Thorfinn's home. Thorfinn managed to refrain from laughing but only just.

"My father and the men of this fiord are down there at the shoreline," Thorfinn pointed to a group of men standing by fishing boats.

"Now we have to walk all the way downhill after walking up hill, let me out of Greenland," complained the tax collector.

Thorfinn conceded that everyone in the Settlement would be only too happy to accommodate his request, by putting him and the priest in boat with a hole in bottom. He would be out of Greenland then.

Moaning and grumbling the two men and their escort trudged down the hill. Thorfinn's father grinned as he watched their approach.

"Here comes our quarry, men. The tithe and taxes seem nicely wrapped up by the old worn walrus hide," commented Thorfinn's father.

"The walrus hide is too good for them, but I couldn't find anything worse," sniggered one man next to Thorfinn's father.

"Shame about that," said Thorfinn's father.

The tax collector puffed out his chest and threw back his head before speaking in haughty manner.

"We have come to collect the King's taxes and Church tithe."

Thorfinn's father kicked the contents wrapped in the walrus hide over to the tax collector's feet.

"That's it," he said rudely.

The priest was set to issue another sermon and excommunication on the men, but when he bent down and unwrapped the hide, his eyes fell on candle sticks and plates of fine quality. The priest gulped. He was ashamed of himself, he had assumed that because the men had behaved in a rough manner, that they weren't Christians or loyal to the King. Yet here was the proof, that the people in the Itivdlek Fiord were the most devout Christians and loyal subjects of the King in the Settlement.

"Bless you my sons. May God protect you and yours now and always," the priest made the sign of the cross.

"I have faith in our God, father," assured Thorfinn's father absolutely enjoying the audacious act he was putting on.

"Oh yes I am sure you have, my son." Then the priest remembered Grimar and asked.

"The orphan boy Grimar wishes to come with us. But if you wish to keep him I would understand. And I know that he would be living in a good Christian home."

Thorfinn's father was of the opinion that Grimar was mad and wished him far away before he committed more insane deeds. Thorfinn had told his father of Grimar's desire to torture an Inuit child, and he suspected a Norse child would be next on Grimar's list. Grimar was a sadistic killer, and children and women would be his main targets as they couldn't fight back. A man who could fight back would be quite safe from Grimar, who was like one of Loki's demons set loose on the world.

"Father, the boy isn't very welcome in the Settlement and it would be best for him if he went. I know that he yearns to work in the fields. He is always talking about fields Father, and there isn't any here," said Thorfinn's father, highly amused at his proposal.

"In that case we had better take him. We are going to the Orkneys and the Earl will find him work in his fields there," assured the priest.

The priest and his escort turned their backs on the group and walked slowly back to the boat. The sailors took their time rowing back to the ship. The priest and his escort climbed up the rope ladder and back on to the ship.

Thorfinn's father and the men with him had to bite down hard on their teeth to prevent an explosion of laughter, and the act caused them discomfort. The priest and the tax collector finally looked away.

Thorfinn's father and his men finally were able to unleash their vent up humor.

The men slapped each other on the back and doubled up in laughed.

"I was nearly busting myself," complained one man.

"Orm the Bold on his raids couldn't have beaten us, men. Did you see the priest's face at the loot he got? He was so impressed with it. And so he should be as it's the Church's own goods. And we got rid of the Grimar boy. I wonder how he will really like working in the fields?" jeered Thorfinn's father thinking he had never had as much fun as he had today. He reached down and grabbed the wonderful finely crafted sword he had taken from the tax collector's feeble assistant.

***

Thorfinn left his father and the men to seek Thor's wisdom, by walking alone on the shoreline.

Some of the crew left the boat to walk on the shoreline.

A sailor walked alone along the shoreline where Thorfinn gazed at the royal ship.

The sailor thought the boy looked like his own son back in Iceland. He stopped to talk with Thorfinn. He asked him how long it would take to reach Iceland, and of the sea around the cape, and the distance to Vinland and how currents had changed since Eric the Red's day, and a ship would need to take a more southerly route, if it wanted to reach Vinland now. The seas were far heavier than in the days of their Viking ancestors. The sailor gave him lessons in sailing on an open sea and the time it took to reach different ports. He told Thorfinn of another ship sailing behind them, and that it could only carry sixty five people at the maximum as it was a smaller ship. He sat with Thorfinn for hours, giving him detailed knowledge of the world beyond Greenland.

In 1315 there had been a great famine in Iceland, and in Europe it had rained and rained, destroying all the crops. The sailor told of the cost in lives and money and how it had accomplished nothing. Peasants had to work for free for the Lord of manor. The Church wanted a tenth of man's income. Two thirds of the land in Iceland was owned by the Church. Abbeys littered the land and gave little back to the people. Wars were being continually fought and at great cost. The poor were the hardest hit. People were burnt alive for heresy against the Church. If the tax collector didn't get you, the Church did. The picture of world without freedom, and being continually robbed by the King and Church didn't sit well in young Thorfinn's mind.

Thorfinn viewed him as a foe, but the sailor had knowledge of the sea and no one in the West Settlement had that anymore. The sailor explained to him about ropes, tar, and nails for the hull of a ship. This was far different to the simply fishing vessels floating across the fiord. Thorfinn took note of the sailor's account of Vinland, ships, and life in Europe.

Vinland, Thorfinn knew, had been lost. Eric the Red and Orm the Bold had sailed to Vinland and traded with the Skraeling—but none of them attacked him. Two female slaves had run away and joined the Skraeling, and came back a year later with their babies. The Skraeling had not harmed them. Eric the Red had been thrown out of Iceland, how could such a man's children get on with the Skraeling? When their father couldn't get on with own people? Eric the Red's daughter killed her own people, but two miserable female slaves managed to get accepted by the Skraeling, so surely someone else could. Thorfinn returned to his father.

***

The priest consulted the tax collector and they paced the deck in contemplation.

"Clearly there are Christian people in the West Settlement, but very few. Just those in the Itivdlek Fiord. The rest are in my opinion out right pagans. If we only had another source of evidence against them other than the boy Grimar, we could go after them. Oh I know they are far away from Norway and the rest of the civilized world—but infection spreads. Make no mistake, once one small area becomes the devil's domain that infection will spread like a fire across all of Christendom and maybe it will break the power of Mother Church. We are an army fighting a never-ending battle against sin for God."

Grimar cringed at the priest's battle cry. Was he going to have to play at being a devoted son of the Church, in order to gain a better life? Grimar paused and realized he couldn't keep up such an act for very long. He hoped the ship would have a speedy journey to Norway. The insipid priest was worse than the tax collector. Being a tax collector would be a good position. He would like to be a tax collector. He could steal and kill—all in the name of King.

"You boy, get to work. Sailors are waiting for a cup of water," the sailor said kicking Grimar.

The priest and the tax collector had their backs to him and couldn't see what was happening. Grimar thought about moaning to them over his vile treatment, but canceled the idea. He had to portray himself as a dutiful son of the Mother Church. He had never been in a church, and no member of his family had either. He didn't even know who Christ was until two days ago. The whole religion sounded stupid to him. Religion and morals were for the weak.

The priest turned round and saw Grimar. He smiled as he walked over to the boy.

"We landed at the farm just beyond the edge of the Itivdlek Fiord. They are true Christians there, and one man told me that you long to work in the fields. I am sure I will be able to arrange that with the Earl of the Orkneys."

Grimar's stunned expression was taken as a sign of unexpected gratitude by the priest. Grimar was disappointed beyond measure; hard work in the fields wasn't the life he wanted. The Thor worshipers had trampled on his plans. He comforted himself with the knowledge that the Earl of the Orkneys was most likely as easy to subdue with sweet words, as was the silly chattering priest. Once in the Orkneys he could charm the Earl into elevating him into a higher position. He had managed to beguile the priest, the Earl couldn't be any harder.

"That is music to me," said Grimar humbly.

The ship's captain frowned and his eyes narrowed as he studied Grimar. He took three strides over the deck and joined the priest.

"The boy seems lazy to me. And I will have none of it on my ship. And sailors dislike a boy who tells tales against his own people. I warn you boy, I will be watching you," warned the captain harshly. He then stomped off.

Grimar tried to be appeared dazed by the accusation and hoped the priest was fooled.

"These sailors are strange folk. But never mind Grimar you will soon be on land," was the only comment Grimar received.

Grimar knew he had succeeded with priest and the tax collector, but why had he failed with the ship's crew? If he wished to dupe men he needed to be able to read them, the same way the priest read his nonsensical Bible. Grimar saw a boat heading towards the ship.

The headman learned of the attacks made by the ship, on the people, and set out in his boat to intercept the ship to demand an explanation. He ordered his men to cut across the bow of the ship.

"Oh it is the chief pagan, the headman," declared the priest.

The headman swung his body over the ship's rail and boarded the ship. His face was face grim, and then he spied Grimar.

"What are you doing here, Grimar?"

"Sailing to the Orkneys with Christian people," replied Grimar doing his best to sound like a devoted Christian, annoyed at living with pagans.

"You are not Christian! You are Grimar the Fool! Grimar the Lazy! Grimar the Liar! The captain here needs to watch you," snorted the headman in mocking laughter.

"Oh I will, rest assured," promised the captain, nodding his head at Grimar.

"I haven't come here about you, Grimar. But the raids on our people! Taking furs needed to keep warm in the winter. Men risk their lives against polar bears to get those furs. We must have them back. And I am here to take them back."

The effrontery of the headman infuriate the priest and the tax collector, they had never had anyone challenge the King and Church in such an open and distasteful manner.

"You will be lodged in the ship and taken back to Norway. You are guilty of treason and heresy," declared the tax collector peering into the headman's eyes.

The headman reeled, his mouth open and his eyes went back in his head, the world around him growing hazy.

"Pillage," he shouted as he raised his old sword. A sharp pain made him clutch his chest, and with a thud, the headman hit the deck.

***

The word was carried across the West Settlement. Their headman died in the defense of his people, trying to stop the pillage. Orm looked to the sky and vowed to be like his father.

"We will remember! We will remember!" shouted Orm with potent anger in his voice.

The royal ship moved from farm to farm snatching furs. The ship moored at one farm after other, seizing furs, ivory and anything else the tax collector considered a due payment to Church and King. The harsh winters, dangerous hunting and isolation hadn't dented their independent pride, but the act of pillage from Mother Church and their devoted King, had plunged them into humiliation and defeat.

The priest's fragile belief in charity and compassion was reserved for those he considered worthy, which was certainly not the savages in the West Settlement of Greenland. Diligently he recorded each item he stole from their humble farms.

At the edge of Lysu Fiord the ship stopped. Ingrid and Thorfinn walked along the shoreline in grief. They felt a surge of pity for the victims of that farm, as the ship sailed towards the cove.

"They are very poor and have only son left to them, all their other children have died. Eric is six years old. Look at the number of wolves gathered to steal from one sick woman and her husband, Thorfinn."

The tax collector pounded the door and burst in without waiting to be invited.

"We have come for the King's taxes and the Church's tithe," declared the tax collector like a trumpet.

A sickly woman dared to ask what the Church and King did with all the stuff. He told her they were sold and converted into silver.

Outraged, she and husband rose from their battered stools and with knives in hand, attacked the priest and the tax collector.

The tax collector's head was only saved when the sailors escorting the pair retaliated and swung an axe into the necks of the man and his wife. Bones crunched, warm blood cascaded from the wounds. Their bodies juddered, pupils dilated, and death's mantle was laid over them. They fell to the hard ground, twitching in the last moments of life.

"Pagans, you will die without absolution," roared the priest as he stood over the twitching bodies at his feet. A boy of six witnessed the affair and cried out, cursing the Church and the King from the doorway.

"Get him, he can join his pagan parents," commanded the priest.

Young Eric took to his heels in terror, with the men in hot pursuit. Tears ran down his face as the men gained ground on him. Eric felt their axes would soon be splitting his neck, just like his parents. Just then he spied Inuit men out hunting and raced towards them.

"Oh please! Oh please!" he begged as he fell on his knees.

Fresh Water's father saw the men hunting the boy, and remembered his young son being hunted down by Grimar; a debt was owed. He signaled with his hand for the boy to join them. Eric was encircled by the Inuit men.

The sailors did not really want to harm the boy, and had only given chase to please the priest, so when they saw the spears in the hands of the Inuit men, they opted to forget the entire episode and walked off.

Eric looked up at Fresh Water's father, and he in turn gazed down at him. Having a Norse child in the camp that could speak the language and know their customs would be a great asset to the tribe, as the Norse were always causing trouble. Their ways were so different from the Inuit where everything was shared. A boy that could walk in the two worlds was a gift to the Inuit.

"For the rest of your life you will be Inuit," announced Fresh Water's father. Six year old Eric walked off with the Inuit hunting party.

***

On a nearby hill top Orm, Thorfinn, and Ingrid watched the sailors who had been chasing down young Eric.

"He is going off with the Skraeling, Ingrid," remarked Thorfinn in shock.

"One day Eric will return, but other paths he will take, and the ground will shake," forecast Ingrid. Orm walked over to where Thorfinn and Ingrid stood.

"If those damn tax collector and priests ever show up again I will be waiting for them," vowed Orm with fists clenched at his side.

"If I see a damn tax collector and a priest come after my goods I will up and go!" vowed Thorfinn with equal determination.

"You will need to be ready for they will return, but in end the seeds of Orm the Bold will saved by the seeds of Orm the bold," stated Ingrid. There was no doubt in her voice.

Orm and Thorfinn failed to heed the warning Ingrid gave.

The next day the ship sailed down the fiord.

"Yea!," jeered angry men and women lined long the shoreline.

"May the ship sink and the King and Church with it!" yelled a youth.

"Yes—sink the Church and King! Sink! Sink!" jeered more people.

The tax collector held his head and took a sip of wine, thanking God he was finally leaving this nest of traitors and heretics. No one had asked the priest with him about confession. He heard mentions of it at one farm, but was sharply told that he was the one in need of confession. Furs had been flung at his feet by men that had the look of a wounded bear. Ivory was thrown onto muddy ground, which had to be extracted and then cleaned. The settlement was a nightmare. The priest who traveled with him gave a soul lifting sermon in the church. Only a handful of Greenlanders showed up, and in the middle of the sermon they walked out. Mother Church was gravely neglected in the West Settlement. He began to ponder on whether these people were really Christians. Or if had they converted back to heathen ways and worshiped the Old Norse Gods? The priest came up to the tax collector at the ship's rail.

"I am so grateful to be leaving this godless land and its heathen people."

"You think they are heathen father?" breathed the tax collector in dismay.

"I am beginning to think this is the case my son," replied the priest in despair, as if he were facing a grave foe.

The worship of the Norse Gods, struck into the heart of the tax collector and the priest. Grimar had proven he was loyal and faithful. And a Christian boy certainly wouldn't want to endanger his soul by living with pagans. The boy was only ten years old and could be mistaken, but the evidence to support his claim was strong.

This terrible revelation had to be presented to the Bishop and the King. It certainly rated an investigation. It would explain the vile actions of the people here. Of course a pagan wouldn't want to support Mother Church. The priest's mind tossed around like the deck he was walking on. Heresy was rearing its evil head across Europe. Its march had to be stopped before the wrath of God descended upon them. The settlement had been founded by Erik the Red and he worshiped the Norse Gods, so it was conceivable that some here had never fully ceased worshiping the Norse Gods. Were they walking on a land full of pagans? St Augustine had said Christ was glorified by the death of pagans. The more the priest thought about the situation, the more he came to the conclusion that Grimar, in spite of his tender years was right. These people were pagans.

The tax collector and the priest felt a burden had been lifted from them as the ship sailed out of the fiord and into the open sea.

"An entire settlement Father—brimming with heretics and rebels."

"Not quite my son remember the men in the Itivdlek Fiord and their generosity to Mother Church and the King. May God bless them and keep them in his tender care."

"There were only ten of them out of a population of over three hundred. Ten decent souls living among rebels and heretics," the tax collector whimpered, slightly shaking his head.

"Ah but my son we have saved one soul and snatched that soul from the den of evil. Young Grimar over there. One soul saved is a glory to God."

The landscape of Greenland faded in the distance.

***

The men gathered at the Sandnes farm felt like a yoke had been lifted from their necks with the ship's departure. Thorfinn's father was the most popular man at the gathering.

"It is a pity I didn't hide away from them more. But like you I didn't think they were such highly skilled robbers," uttered Thorfinn's father. Embarrassed by words of flattery, he considered his actions to be just the Norse way of looking after kin.

Just as the ships swung south, a rogue wave hit the smaller ship accompanying the larger royal vessel, and sailors were washed over-board and drowned. The ship was seen sailing west on its side.

The priest crossed himself. The devil was at work. The pagans had conjured up the devil's brew and sunk the ship. It was fortunate he was on board the main ship else it too would have been sunk. The devil had no power against a man of the cloth.

Thorfinn's father watching the ship topple on its side and smiled with delight.

"Thank you Thor."

Ingrid came up behind him and sighed.

"I asked Thor to sink both of them. He only granted part of my wish? Don't know why Thor didn't sink both of their ships."

"Because Thor wishes one of them to reach Norway for a reason you and I will never know Ingrid."

Ingrid trotted off thinking about what Thorfinn's father had said.

"Well Thor, if you wished that ship to get back to Norway I guess you want one to return one day."

Ingrid prayed to Thor and vowed to follow him all of her days.

A voice inside of Ingrid told her that ships would sail for the seeds of Orm the Bold.

Ingrid shook her head. She had no understanding of the message given to her. Seeds bequeathed by a very distant Viking ancestor, who was the ancestor of Thorfinn and Orm, and many thousands of others who lived in far off England and Scotland? The premonition faded. Ingrid tried to capture its careless interlude in her mind, but failed. She looked down at Astrid in her arms and smiled.

"You will know more than me, my little Astrid and be more powerful than your mother. Bjarni, I know you are with Odin now in Valhalla. But I do wish you were here with me. Bjarni watch over Astrid. Maybe she will wed Thorfinn. He seems as if he will grow into a warrior. I like Thorfinn very much. Why didn't any of my trances warn me of the Christians though, and the tax collector that came to kill you? Did I offend Thor? Is that why Bjarni wasn't saved? I can't think how I offended Thor. I would make amends if I have. Bjarni, why did you have to die and leave me?"

Ingrid wallowed in grief as she carried Astrid over the hill tops and down the valley to Sandnes farm, hoping Orm would give her a home. She couldn't bear to stay alone anymore in her one room house.

Ingrid walked into the great hall at Sandnes farm and found Orm seated at the table.

"Orm you can have my farm, if you will but let me live here…"

"There is no need to ask Ingrid, you can't stay there alone. I will be a man like my father, and I think little Astrid will be like you."

"I hope Thorfinn will marry Astrid one day. He would make Astrid a good husband Orm."

"Did you hear any more about the boy Eric, Ingrid?"

"Eric is with the Inuit and has become a Inuit for a time."

"I am still a Christian…but the Church must reform. I will be waiting with a sword in hand for any Royal ships that come calling and find out whether not they have reformed," chuckled Orm. The weight of being the headman fell heavy on his young shoulders.

"The church will be reformed. But not by its own hand," predicted Ingrid grimly.

Astrid began to walk. Her hair was sliver blonde like her mother's and her wide blue eyes gazed up at Orm.

"Perhaps Astrid will marry Halfdan?" suggested Orm in a happy carefree mood.

"She will be sixteen summers old before she inherits my gifts, and will not marry before then," warned Ingrid the Wise.

Astrid had been dedicated to Thor, and Thor alone would choose Astrid's husband. The man would carry the seed of Einar of the Orkneys and be a modern day Viking; a warrior skilled battle, loyal, brave and highly adaptable. Eric came into her mind, surely not him though thought Ingrid? Thor gave no further insight into the future.

Freda entered the hall and with a casual laugh that indicated she wasn't really expecting an answer, asked Ingrid a question.

"What gifts will Halfdan inherit?"

Ingrid eyes were glazed as she replied.

"It is you,who will give a great inheritance to your son and to a modern Viking."

Freda's stifled laughter lay in her chest. There were no Vikings anywhere in the world; all the Vikings had died out centuries ago, and she had nothing much to give.

Ingrid departed and left Freda smirking at Orm.

"Vikings..really Orm?"

Orm didn't discount Ingrid's prediction, he analyzed the meaning of the word 'Viking' and reached the terrible conclusion that Ingrid meant. The man was going to be a replica of Orm the Bold or Einar of the Orkneys.

Orm thought about the saga of Orm the Bold. His ancestor wasn't a Christian. All his female slaves came out of convents; their description of Christianity was the only thing that struck terror into Orm the Bold. He never lost a battle. So Orm was baffled as to why Orm the Bold was bothered about the church? Orm the Bold fought for land rather than gold and silver. The Skraeling traded with him and honored him. Orm the Bold had twenty one children. His descendants could well occupy land in Iceland, the Orkneys, Scotland, England, and maybe even Vinland. Orm the Bold and Einar who took the Orkneys, were the only Vikings mentioned by Ingrid. Orm safely assumed these two men were her idea of a Viking. But saintly Freda had nothing to offer men, like Einar of the Orkneys and Orm the Bold. Ingrid's mind must be affected by the death of her husband.

"Freda, I think Ingrid is still ill."

"Yes, I doubt there are any men like that about. Young Thorfinn would be the closest. Einar of the Orkneys was run down by his father, yet he was the one who got rid of all his father's foes. So Ingrid is wrong, and you are right she is in mourning. What about Grimar though, I am pleased he has gone.'

"Maybe in a warmer land, he will recover," said Orm optimistically.

**

The Royal ship docked in the Orkneys. The priest and the tax collector abandoned the boy into the care of the local Priest Father Olav, who chatted to the captain about the boy before he took Grimar to the Earl.

In the great hall, the Earl of the Orkneys gave Grimar a few moments of his precious time. He had to cope with the King's tax collector, who had shown up with the ship from Greenland. Providence was kind, the King's tax collector was over-wrought by his visit to Greenland, and far too upset to poke his nose into the Orkney's smuggling business. Hopefully he would stay distracted,until the nuisance sailed off.

"My lord Earl—this boy is from Greenland where there are no crops and he has a great yearning to work in the fields. Out of charity I implore you my lord to allow the boy a place here in the Orkneys and to work in the fields," asked Father Olav humbly and quietly waited for the Earl to reach a decision.

"He doesn't look at all pleased with the charity I am being asked to bestow!" bellowed the Earl as he put down his goblet on the table.

Grimar's sour face suddenly transformed into a more sedate and grateful pose, but it was too late. The Earl wasn't taken in by Grimar's quick transformation.

The steward entered and bowed.

"My Lord?" asked the steward.

"This boy seems to think he is too good to work in my fields, steward."

"My lord your fields are too good for him. With my lord's permission I will see to that he gets a good beating and then is assigned to the cesspit."

"An excellent idea! Take it away," the Earl a waved lazy hand at Grimar.

Grimar was dragged out by the scruff of his neck, given a beating outside the great hall, and then put to work in the cesspit.

While working in the filth and stench, he heard talk of Scotland, a land that was only miles away by a small boat. Later he learnt that one of the kitchen girls came from Scotland, Grimar made friends with her, and asked her to teach him the language of Scotland.

Revenge wove its magic in Grimar's psychotic mind, he would teach the West Settlement to jeer at him and use him for amusement. They would be made to pay for what they did to him. The haughty Earl would pay too, for the beating and work he had been forced to undertake. First he would learn to speak the language of Scotland, and then find a place there. But Grimar did stop to ponder on what kind of a report the tax collector would give on his return to Norway?

The tax collector issued a damning report to the King about his rebellious subjects in the West Settlement of Greenland, and how his very life had been threatened, and that not one person had attempted to pay any tax, but wanted the King to pay them money for their goods. "Trade not taxes", cried the people of Greenland's

West Settlement. The King was shocked. If this got out other subjects would take it into their heads not to pay taxes.

The Bishop almost choked on his French wine when he read of the heresy breeding up in the West Settlement of Greenland. It was a pity the only witness was a ten year old boy. A careful record of the event in 1327 was put away, advising that if any man in future made such a claim the people were to be exterminated as heretics.

1342

Grimar was running over the rocks with the sea pounding below. Men with double edged axes were closing in on their quarry. The Highlander men were better runners and fighters than Grimar. His mind was unhinged with terror. It would be death if they found him and not a quick one either.

Dark clouds were gathering, Grimar prayed for rain. Only sheets of cold rain could halt their manhunt. He briefly looked down at the beach below. Grim Highlanders were pacing the sand, waiting like prowling wolves for him to try and make a dash for the boat that lay on the beach. The boat represented a trip out of Scotland, away from the clutches of the Sinclair clan. The boat could take him to the Orkneys where Norway ruled. He had to reach that boat. A flash of lighting lit up the beach and the sharp blades of the Highlanders. Grimar shuddered at the sight of those gleaming blades and the thought of the blades craving into his flesh.

The Highlanders to his horror, took shelter from the gathering storm in the very boat he wished to use. Their comrades had taken shelter in the caves. The sea offered no escape for Grimar.

He looked at the dark hidden forest behind him. Trees and bushes were alien to Grimar, he felt that demons and ghosts lived in the dense green and brown domain. But it was the only route open to him and he had to take it, even if he didn't know where the forest would lead to. Nothing could be worse than waiting for the axe wielding Highlanders to come and get him. Grimar had to slide on his belly in mud to reach the forest. The wind whistling though the branches reminded him of Greenland.

The life he dreamed of in Christendom had been denied him, because of Thorfinn's father telling that prattling pious priest he wanted to work in the fields. The Earl of Orkneys took a dislike to him from the moment he was presented to the Earl, and with a wave of the Earl's hand, he had been condemned to work in the cesspit. The only comfort he had was the fact the Orkneys was warmer. People shunned him in the Orkneys, just as they had in Greenland. So he stole a boat and moved to Scotland and now he had to move back to the Orkneys. Nothing was going right for him. He couldn't stay long in the Orkneys, the people would remember him and the Earl was cunning man. The rain blocked out his vision, drenching his clothes and body.

Huddled in the trees Grimar tried to plot a way out of his dilemma. He shivered but he was also relieved he could no longer hear the sound of hunters. All through the night he kept a watch out for demons in the forest. The cursed landscape of Northern Scotland was covered in frightening forests. The Orkneys hardly possessed any of the frightening spectacles.

The morning light whipped up more fear in Grimar, as he knew the hunt for him would be resumed, by the rough and tough Sinclair clan. He ran like mad through the forest, falling on the ground, getting cut by sharp pickles from the underground. His skin was a mass of cuts and bruises, when he saw light bursting in between the trees. An open meadow lay before him and a tiny beach. Grimar's heart lifted when his line of vision came to rest on a boat.

Grimar walked casually down to the beach. A boy standing by a boat became alarmed to see a stranger heading towards him. Grimar placed his knife behind his back, as he approached the worried boy. The boy moved to the side quickly, saw the knife and ran. Grimar opted not to chase after him. It was the boat he wanted. He pushed the boat out into the water and jumped in. Inside the boat Grimar started to relax. He could escape now.

Horsemen galloped onto the beach. Grimar's mouth gaped in horror at Highlanders armed with board swords, rushing through the sea to get him. He applied all his strength to the oars. The wind picked up the sail and took him out to sea. He gave a loud mocking laugh as he watched the frustrated Highlanders up to their knees in water, their horses unable to swim out; the brutes couldn't get him.

"Never mind men, there is only one place he can be heading for. The Orkneys. And the Earl is friend to our Laird. There is a larger vessel leaving for the Orkneys, we will ask the captain of the vessel to let the Earl know we want this Grimar," comforted the leader of the men.

Grimar landed his boat in the Orkneys ahead of the sailing vessel. He saw a Royal ship anchored off the coast and decided to try to gain passage. To Grimar's relief the ship was short of crew, so he was granted passage as a sailor. He was overjoyed to learn the ship was sailing to Norway. He struck up a friendship with a sailor, who had lived in Iceland and Grimar began to spin tales into the sailor's head about Greenland.

In Norway Grimar and the sailor went ashore. As they walked along the waterfront Grimar informed the sailor of the practices he had seen in the West Settlement; the worshiping of the Norse Gods. In a tavern by the waterfront, Grimar plied jugs of ale down the sailor's throat and the sailor began to shout about the pagan practices of the people in the West Settlement of Greenland. Grimar quietly left the tavern without being noticed.

The church authorities soon heard about the incident at the tavern and the man was brought before the Bishop. The sailor fearing for his own safety, stuck to his story. The Bishop recalled the incident in 1327 and Grimar's testimony.

Grimar wisely waited for the sailor's ship to leave Norway, before he approached a priest with his old accusation that he had made as a child, and how his conscious was troubling him. The priest notified the Bishop, who went down on his knees and thanked God that a second witness was in Norway. He had Grimar brought before him. Grimar repeated the tale he had spun sixteen years earlier. The Bishop asked Grimar's pardon for having doubted his testimony, and told Grimar that a sailor had come forth with the same terrible story. Two witnesses coupled the damning report, of 1327 which resulted in the proclamation that the West Settlement of Greenland was full of heretics. The Bishop looked through his list of priests and wondered who was the most expendable. Ivar's name appeared on the list. If he drowned at sea or was killed in Greenland, it would be no loss to the church. He would send Grimar with him. Grimar knew the people, and had nobly offered to go; the act of a true Christian man. The priest Ivar protested to the Bishop at being sent on such a horrid mission. A offer of a post in the far north of Norway however, brought the priest round to accept the mission. The Bishop dressed up the mission as a holy undertaking, with an ample reward for success, to boost Ivar's frail disposition.

The Bishop paced up and down in his luxurious palace, thinking of who he could get to carry out the extermination of the West Settlement of Greenland. English archers came to mind. The men didn't speak Norse and had no connections to Norse people. Employing men from Norway, Iceland, or the Orkneys wouldn't be wise. In Iceland the church was getting a bad review. Trusting any Norseman was too risky. The English archers had the worst reputation since the Vikings. They were ideal.

A ship was dispatched to England to hire English archers, the most deadly warriors of their day.

The Emissary and Grimar sailed to England and met with an English priest. They told him only of the need to hire archers to go to Greenland where the Skraeling was a grave problem. He informed Ivar of a young archer had just drunk the church's wine and was about to be hung for his terrible crime. His fellow archers were furious. The priest decided that this group of men were the prefect individuals for his brother priest from Norway to employ. He made the archers a offer of employment in the service of the King of Norway and passage to Greenland with good pay. Their comrade would hang if they refused.

The leader Mark readily accepted. Greenland sounded like a nice place and all they had to do was guard the church Emissary from enemies. His friend Peter was absent as he was busy praying to Saint Ann in a local church. When Peter joined his comrades he seemed very pleased with the employment offer.

Captain Harkonson was the ship's captain and with a crew of just over twenty, the voyage to Greenland began. The Captain spoke English and welcomed the English archers aboard his ship. The Emissary and Grimar received only a formal welcome from the Captain. He thought the church was very foolish to undertake paying archers for protection against the Skraeling, just to check on church property that was not worth having. Nothing in Greenland was worth having.

The sail was hoisted and the ship set off for Greenland.

THE WEST SETTLEMENT'S SORROW

Orm held the title of headman in the West Settlement and stood looking down at the Lysu Fiord. It was clear of ice floes for now. The worst winter they had ever faced finally loosened its crushing grip. All the children under eight had died. All the pregnant women had also perished. The population of the West Settlement was two hundred and ten, only seventy were children. His heart and mind churned in misery and grief. He could barely hold back the tears. The West Settlement was the last of the King of Norway's domains. No ship had visited in sixteen years and even then it had only came to plunder. At thirty three he was leathered skinned and white haired, the oldest person in the Settlement. Only his wife's mother had lived into old age.

This Settlement could no longer sustain them, it had to be abandoned. This summer too. Boats were made of driftwood and skin, that had to make the two hundred and fifty mile journey to the East Settlement. It was a terrible voyage for such simple boats to sail.

The East Settlement folk had never been friendly in the past. Hunting had been done at great risk and the profits were taken by the East Settlement folk. The Norse way of sharing wasn't practiced by them. Trade and money was what they cared about.

Orm studied the fiord and ever encroaching ice cliffs. No amount of trade or money would influence the ice cliffs' advance. Nature's wrath was approaching more fiercely than any army, bearing down on its foe. Orm's weary thoughts turned to Thorfinn and his people in the Itivdlek Fiord.

The people in the Itivdlek Fiord were planning on going to Vinland. A four hundred mile journey across an open sea. Thorfinn was the best sailor in the Settlement, but he had never faced an open sea. Certainly the Vikings had done it, but not with the flimsy vessels they possessed. Thorfinn and his followers had prayed and prayed to the Norse God, but Thor was deaf to Thorfinn's pleas. Orm flung a trip to Vinland out of his head; a journey to the East Settlement commanded his thoughts.

A voyage to the East Settlement was the only route open to them and from there they would have to try and get passage to Iceland. There was no other alternative. With a heavy heart facing the prospect of a very arduous voyage and the high chance of drowning at sea, Orm walked down the slope to the edge of the shoreline. The two young men that waited there were equally as grim as Orm.

Orm put his fist to his mouth and spoke with immense grief. He protested against the hardship of his life. Four thousand people once lived in the West Settlement. Last summer there were four hundred—now only two hundred and ten people remained.

"Men, take a message round the Settlement. This Settlement must be abandoned this summer. I suggest we take boats and sail to the East Settlement and from there take passage out of Greenland. This land will no long support us and I doubt it will support the East Settlement for much longer either. Look at those ice cliffs—they grow taller and near. We must leave while we can, if we stay another winter we may not be able to leave."

Orm's pronouncement was only what the young men thought themselves and it came as no surprise. Clinging to a life in the West Settlement was to clutch at death.

"Think you will find everyone is in agreement. We have to go. Death is all that awaits anyone who lives here," sneered one young man.

Orm walked along the shoreline casting his eyes over the battered boats that would have to make the two hundred and fifty mile journey to the East Settlement. Every piece of drift wood would be needed to repair the boats and make them sea worthy for such a hard voyage. Should he forget about sailing there and walk instead? It may take longer but it could be safer. Orm's chest constricted at the empty defeat that may await him with either choice.

"God or Thor won't you at least save our young?" pleaded Orm. He felt as if he was drowning under the weight of obstacles and uncertainty. For three hundred years Norse people had lived in this land, who would have forecast such a dire outcome as the one the whole Settlement now faced? Gone were the green meadows where once cattle gazed. Ships came to collect precious ivory, which wasn't wanted anymore. Viking ships had cut across an ocean and conquered plenty of lands. Except the land to the far west, full to the brim with food and warmth, it had a draw back—the thousands of Skraeling that lived there. Neither the King of Norway nor any other King would conqueror that land. No king in Europe had an army large enough to conqueror Vinland.

"Why didn't we leave earlier, why didn't we heed the warning signs,?" sighed Orm in despair.

Halfdan and Astrid strolled along the edge of the fiord. They argued loudly as they walked along, stopping now and then to face one another, firing up their row to a greater intensity.

Orm breathed hard and released a grumble, his angry eyes resting on the two trouble makers. An evacuation had to be carried out under dangerous conditions, and the Bible preacher and the 'warm- island' preacher were having yet another verbal battle at the top of their lungs. The two youths pulled down their bottom lips and fled for the boat. Orm didn't blame them, he wanted to take the boat and leave too.

"I have been praying to the Saints. Have faith and all will be well. More praying is what the Settlement must do. And trying to convert Thorfinn, his people, and the Inuit to Christ! If this were done God would send ships to take us out of Greenland," shouted Halfdan in the voice of a youthful devotee.

"I have prayed to the Saints and to Thor just be safe. And a ship is coming to take me to a warm-island with castles. Not the East Settlement. Not Iceland or Norway, Halfdan," she said. Astrid's voice was full of unshakable faith.

Orm put his hand on his head. His son and his ward Astrid were just as mad as each other. Neither of them gave a man any peace. And he needed peace in order to plan a very dangerous journey. Both of them thought a miracle was going to occur; none had in the last sixteen years. Thor and the Saints must be deaf or asleep. They had to think about saving themselves. Prayers to any God may well go unheard. Did the two great mouth-movers realize that the weather had no ears to hear and no eyes to see?

Halfdan and Astrid came within a few yards of where Orm stood muddling over his options; lives depended on him getting it right. His emotional dam broke and Orm bellowed out.

"Quiet you pair of pests! You are both asking for a miracle of epic portions."

Orm was conscious of the fact that it was going to take an act of God to save the people of the West Settlement. Faith in any God was ebbing away. Were his children going to die a slow death in Greenland? Was there no future for his children, just death? Had his foolish ancestors sentenced them to death, with their desire to be free and own land? Freedom was a cry echoed throughout Norse lands. Thousands had fled to Iceland to be free and ten thousand here to Greenland. It was possible to die of shame, Orm felt he could. For that is how he felt, ashamed. He was scared by the history and the events of 1327, and the prospect of a two hundred and fifty mile dangerous journey that had to be made. Orm burst into an explosive rage and roared at Halfdan and Astrid again.

"Halfdan why don't you go hunting or fishing with your friend Fresh Water for the next six days? While I sought out sailing plans! We have to leave this land. Meet me at pointed rocks. Now go you pest. And you girl, go and collect driftwood now!"

The pair stopped arguing as they realized they had gone too far. Halfdan saw the trip as an opportunity to go and preach God's word. Astrid took the order to collect wood as a chance to plea with Thor again to find out when the ship would arrive. Thor had sent a ship; it was on its way and would soon arrive.

"Oh Mighty Thor I do thank thee and wish to forget Greenland and all its horrors," mumbled Astrid, out of Halfdan's hearing. Astrid had washed herself of Christianity, she was now like her mother before her; a follower of the Norse Gods. Ingrid's gift had taken its first infant cry inside Astrid.

Orm felt some relief as his priest-like son was heading for a boat. Halfdan stopped at the water's edge and went to up Astrid. He placed her necklace round her neck.

"Wear it, you will need it," said Halfdan. He didn't know why Astrid needed the cross.

"I will share my gift with you, the one my mother gave to me, Halfdan. Oh and take the runes also." Astrid gave the tiny pouch full of runes to Halfdan.

Astrid was about to pluck the ivy Christian cross from her neck but an odd sensation made her pause, her hand fell at her side, and she left the cross hanging around her neck.

Orm watched them depart. Thorfinn's farm would be his son's first port of call before he went off to hunt with Fresh Water. It was a horrid thing to do to Thorfinn, who was his friend. But he had to have peace. Abandoning the Settlement was a serious undertaking. And if Astrid returned, prattling about life in a warm-island with castles again, she could go and live with her cousins. Now there were two men he wouldn't be consulting. They were nearly as mad as Grimar the Fool. It was the first time Orm had thought of Grimar in years. Perhaps Grimar wasn't such a fool—he was living in a warm land. Not cold Greenland. Thorfinn and he were the fools. Thorfinn surpassed Astrid with his dreams of living in Vinland. A dose of Halfdan's preaching would do Thorfinn the world of good.

Freda saw her son Halfdan was about to leave and called for him to wait. Halfdan waited until his mother reached his boat.

"My son, remember what I told of your grandmother."

Halfdan thought it odd that his mother should mention his

grandmother on this occasion. That woman must have been truly mad. The tales she told his mother.

"Remember her tales, Halfdan."

"Yes but they were such stories, mother. She had just heard about Vinland and made the rest up. Nobody on the ship in 1294 brought anything back but wood."

"Give this map to Thorfinn, Halfdan. It is from the ship in 1294. Give his people a fighting chance. And take my mother's charm— put it around your neck." Freda handed a map to Halfdan.

"I will do that as I have no use for either. The old world is for me mother, not some place with people who have no books and no civilizations. I could go live with the Inuit if I want that."

Halfdan walked off in good humor as he was one never to bear grudges. Freda, with tired eyes and grief born of suffering, cried to a woman who died many years ago.

"Oh mother were all your stories just that...stories? Or were they really about you and your people? I grow weary and my life is drawing to a close. So I ask God, or Thor, or the spirit of my mother, to watch over my sons...deliver them and their children. Ingrid... oh how I wish I had your sight."

Astrid heard her words as she put one foot in her boat. Astrid stopped and walked back to where Freda stood on the wet stony shoreline. A distant look shone in Astrid's eyes, her voice was somber, with a ring of certainty in her words.

"Your sons live and tread a path beyond your wildest dreams, Freda."

At that moment Astrid's eyes looked so like her mother's. Had Ingrid passed on her sight to her daughter? Freda sought to ask more questions about where Halfdan was going. Iceland would suit well. There was hot water for asking there. The church would be sure to welcome him. An alternative thought entered her head. Halfdan wasn't going to be a priest. That would suit her husband nicely - he hated the idea of Halfdan being a priest. After all he couldn't marry nor have children.

"What paths will Olaf take and Halfdan, Astrid?"

Astrid's face changed. Her mother's gift had left her for the moment.

She shook her head and her mouth opened slightly; the girl was so foolish. A warm-island, a dream so far-fetched, once more flowered in her voice.

"A warm-island." Astrid strolled back to her boat to go and search for driftwood.

"Oh God or Thor do wake her up to the real world," yelled Freda to the sky. For just an instant, Astrid had held her mother's power, but it was short lived, the craze for a warm-island had soon over taken her. Thorfinn at least had a chance of getting to Vinland. Crazy Astrid had no chance.

Olaf came walking down the hill. His fail body and thin legs brought tears to her eyes. Greenland was going to kill him if she didn't get him out of the place before the next winter.

"Olaf go and rest," commanded Freda, full of worry.

"Mother I can walk a little now. I am getting stronger. And I am eight years old you know."

"Is Astrid talking about her warm-island again, Mother?"

"Yes...a magical ship is coming just to take Astrid to a warm-island."

Olaf giggled. He too wanted to live in place where there was castles, roads, and markets, but the place didn't have to be a warm-island. He was more realistic at eight than silly Astrid was at sixteen. Olaf thought it odd Astrid's mother had been called wise. Her daughter should be called Astrid the dreamer.

"Thorfinn won't like a visit from Halfdan." Olaf walked off.

Freda thought of Thorfinn and his voyage to Vinland. Four hundred miles by sea. The vessel would sink on the first hurdle of waves. Were they all doomed? Were sickly Olaf and Halfdan going die with her in the coming winter? Freda cried out against her cruel fate. Thorfinn was right to die trying, rather than waiting here for a slow cold death. Freda pleaded once more, this time for Thor to save her sons.

"Orm the Bold, if your spirit can hear me take my plea to Thor;

save my sons, save your descendants!" Freda screamed to a cloud floating across the sky, her tears fell as she asked for a miracle, from the God her ancestors had long ago abandoned.

Thorfinn was lodged in stillness. He had prayed to Thor for the wood, iron, and knowledge to build a ship. He freely acknowledged that he had asked a tremendous favor of Thor, and logs had already been sent. Thorfinn trembled even more when he discovered a battered ship washed on the shoreline of his farm. When the passion of finding such a marvel finally died down, Thorfinn managed to take stock of the rich bounty Thor had passed into his hands. Thorfinn fell on his knees in the wet gray sandy beach.

"Oh mighty Thor honour and glory is yours and we thank you for this bounty that is beyond what we deserve. It is a fabulous gift you have given this day, and just after giving those beautiful logs you sent us last week. Oh mighty Thor praise be to your name," Thorfinn then recalled the curse Ingrid had placed on the ships from Norway. This ship wreck was the smaller of the King's ships. Ingrid's curse was their salvation.

"Oh Ingrid thank you—I will save your daughter. She will be on this ship. I will not leave her here to die. Astrid will be saved," vowed Thorfinn with all sincerity.

Humbled and shaken by Thor's act, Thorfinn put himself into a work regime. Three planks had suffered a beating from the sea. Other than that the ship appeared to be in good order. His younger brother had also seen the shipwreck and was charging down the slope to look at Thor's wondrous gift.

"Praise be to Thor! What a find! How much damage has it suffered? Where did it come from?" rattled eighteen year old Noddad. His blonde curly ringlets formed a fizzy bush of hair around his blue eyes. His stout body stood against the wind whipping round the fiord.

Noddad's rapid questions, coaxed Thorfinn out of his euphoric mood. A more thorough examination of the ship was necessary.

"I have to climb on board to check the damage. You may have to pull me out if I fall through the deck, Noddad."

Thorfinn acted as if the wood were gold when he touched the mast. He couldn't find a single splitter in the wooden mast. It was totally intact. The sail was gone and canvas sail was impossible make in Greenland. Skins would have to sew together by the women to make a sail. It would be a labour intensive job, but Thorfinn had complete faith in his wife and other women to make a strong flexible sail.

He turned his mind back to 1327 when he asked a sailor how many people the ship would carry. Sixty five maximum had been the answer. In the fiord where he lived everyone were followers of the Norse Gods, except for Grimar's cousins and no God would want them. There were six men, four women and eight children.

Thorfinn pushed back his blonde hair. Deck took his weight and there were no splitters in the wood.

Noddad had never seen a ship of this size and weight. To him the ship appeared to be capable of sailing all the way to Norway. The lure of the Old Norse World began to dig into his soul. Should he try and talk Thorfinn into making the longer and harder voyage back to Iceland or maybe even the Orkneys? Thor had given so much. Would he not calm the seas and allow them to go home?

"Thorfinn is the ship strong enough to make the journey to the homelands?" Noddad asked rather timidly, knowing that his brother's heart was set on Vinland.

Anger flared up instantly in Thorfinn's eyes. His young bother had never seen a real ship like the one in 1327. This one was its inferior, to implore Thor to keep the sea calm for a crossing to Vinland was more than enough. He for one didn't intend to invoke Thor's anger by asking for the safe passage to the Norse homeland. This ship simply wasn't capable of making that voyage. Thorfinn grew suspicious—was this desire to reach the homeland something to do with Noddod's desire for Astrid?

Noddad was besotted with the sixteen year old Astrid, daughter of Ingrid the Wise, who was blessed with her mother's silvery blonde hair, high cheek bones, blue eyes, and wide hips. She possessed none of her mother's famous insight. And that was what impressed Thorfinn about Ingrid. All the settlement had heard of Astrid's desire to live in a warm island with castles. This ship wouldn't make such journey. Astrid would have to be very exalted for Thor to grant such an outrageous request.

"I have seen a Royal ship. This one is only half the size and so it has half the strength. It can't make it round Cape Farewell. We have to go to Vinland because it is the only place we can go, Noddad"

His brother admitted to himself Astrid was the real reason why he wished to sail back to the homeland. Astrid would come with him if he did.

Thorfinn thoughts returned to studying the wreck.

"I wonder where it came from," Noddad asked as he forgot his desire. A metal emblem was attached to the side of the ship which told them where it came from.

"It is one of the two ships that came here in 1327. Astrid's mother put a curse on the ships for them to sink before they reached Norway and sink it did. Ingrid followed the Norse Gods. I have a feeling that the other ship got back to Norway though," admitted Thorfinn unhappy at the thought. He feared a second visit by a Royal ship. Thorfinn was at a loss to think why, until he recalled Ingrid's warning that the second ship would hold Viking warriors. Thorfinn thought of Ingrid's cryptic message and dismissed it— there were no Vikings left. Not a single army in Christendom could fight like a Viking, and Ingrid made that prediction on her deathbed. He felt very safe from any Viking raid. Besides the West Settlement didn't have anything worth raiding. His Vikings ancestors would never have raided such a worthless place. If any Viking saw modern day Greenland, not a Viking shoe would have stepped ashore.

Thorfinn's sharp eyes saw the sadness in brother's eyes, and conceded that Noddad would be miserable without Astrid.

"She is an orphan and lives with Orm. Just go and take her, it's for her own good. And she drifts between Christianity and Norse Gods due to her mother's teachings. And I have vowed to save Ingrid's daughter for without her mother's curse we wouldn't have this ship. We owe it to Ingrid to save Astrid, from herself," Thorfinn emphasized the last word with a heaving snarl.

The news brought instant cheer to Noddad. Astrid was just a sixteen year old and a female. She really didn't know what was best for her. He would follow Orm the Bold's tactics and just take her and put her on the ship. Noddad felt a load of worry had been lifted from him. Astrid, Vinland, and new life would all his. Once in Vinland Astrid would soon laugh at the thought of a 'warm island' with castles.

"You are right Thorfinn. I will just take her."

An uneasy sensation came over Thorfinn as his brother's confident words rang in his ears. The imagines of Ingrid, Eric, and Grimar came to mind. Ingrid had died when Astrid was ten, leaving her daughter caught between two conflicting religions. Halfdan added to Astrid's wandering state of mind, by teaching her to read from the only book in the West Settlement, a book on stupid Saints. Instead of being influence by the religious stories, Astrid became enthralled with the cities and markets she read about. The lifestyle of those people seemed much more appealing to her than life in Greenland. Orm, in the hope of clearing her head had told her, the saga of Orm the Bold. His exploits had filled her with yearning for a land she had never seen. Ingrid had insights and was with one with Thor, Astrid was not. An existence in Christendom would be too hard for Astrid. She had no dowry and no great skills. The silly girl would end up starving, even if she got there. Noddad could provide and protect her. Astrid couldn't do any better.

Thorfinn dismissed Astrid from his thoughts the ship was too important to be worrying about a sixteen year old girl.

"Look what's coming," Noddad pointed to boats with four men rowing hard and in straight line for the gray beach. Children and women were also in the boats.

"Our men and families," shouted Thorfinn, his heart beating wildly.

His neighbors were flocking to the beach where the ship had washed up. Except for Astrid's cousins, whose farm was at the very edge of the fiord. Thorfinn wasn't expecting them to show up for work and didn't want the mad creatures.

"Thorfinn we saw the ship! Is it repairable?" shouted a man anxiously from the boat.

"Yes," shouted Thorfinn with a grin on his face.

Deep bellowing sounds echoed off the cliffs and men pulled hard at the oars. The men nearly fell into the cold water in the rush to examine the cherished object.

Noddad had gone back on board the ship and was fretting around when he noticed barrels and a chest. He broke one the chest with an ivory blade. The sight within the chest made him fall to his knees. "Mighty Thor your gift is more than we are worth!"

Thorfinn and the men gazed upward and wondered what Noddad had found.

"Nails, and they are not rusty—we can make the ship worthy," his voice shook, as he released his thundering announcement.

Thorfinn fell on knees. He could scarcely believe the people who came to rob them, were inadvertently going to save them and had left equipment behind. Thor's plans were too hard for a lowly man such as himself to follow. One man held out his arms and squeezed his fists as he pounded the air in his joy.

"Let it get to work we are wasting sunlight and insulting Thor with laziness. We must sail before the winter sets in. Every child under seven died last winter and every pregnant woman died too. We must leave Loki's domain," pronounced Thorfinn with grim conviction.

"How many can the ship take, Thorfinn?" asked one of the youths. All the men looked to Thorfinn with anxious hearts. He was the only one who could really remember what a sea going vessel looked like and how many people a ship could support.

Thorfinn turned very serious and breathed heavily prior to making his very brutal forecast.

"Sixty five maximum and there are eighteen of us. We will have to leave behind everything. Barrels that can be filled with water and cooked seal meat are all we can take. The ship must not be weighed down. Vinland is a land of plenty. We don't need anything from here. We must save as many people as we can."

"I agree. This is a wonderful gift."

"No more long dark winters. I know there are those who are afraid of the Skraeling. But remember the tales of William of England he harried the north and thousands died. How can we know there isn't a war going on? And Iceland has had famine. The East folk hate us. We could easily starve. And Erik the Red couldn't get on with his own people. His daughter was rotten. But just because they couldn't get on with the Skraeling doesn't mean we can't," voiced one man, totally convinced that a journey to the home lands, would not bring them anything. They would have no land, no trade. In fact they had nothing anyone would want in the home lands. The King and the Church were two things they didn't want and both were there.

"I intend to travel steadily down the coastline until we find a friendly tribe of Skraeling. We can do it slowly. Without having to go far out to sea. Stop for a while and see if we like the land, and if we do move on. We have a ship."

The men nodded in agreement. The idea was sound and to use the ship as a home until they found a better one was wise.

"The warm sun on my back appeals to me and to my wife who is with child," announced one man.

"This another reason to go men. We have lost so many of our women in childbirth. There will soon be none left if we don't go. And I know two of you, like my brother, have no wives. The Skraeling will look more kindly on us if some of us are married to their women. There is no better alliance than one by blood," pronounced Thorfinn.

The desperate single men were completely cheered by the news. Marriage would ensure acceptance, and a family was their hearts desire. A man without a family had no future to their way of thinking. Magnus lugged a log with the aid of four other men, and thought of a wife and mother for his ten year old son.

"I am going to abduct Astrid for her own good," stated Noddad adamantly.

The men hailed Noddad on and hoped he would succeed. They couldn't foresee any obstacles to his plan of action. The consent of Astrid herself eluded them. She was a girl of sixteen—her views didn't count. Noddad was a good hunter, fisherman, a fighter and sailor...what more could a girl want in a husband?

Thorfinn was considering spreading the word of his find and turned to the men gathering up the axes to chop wood.

"Men, I am considering spreading the word of our find and idea. We can take forty more to Vinland with us. Fifteen would have to be men. We could sail back to collect the rest?"

"I don't see any of them here trying to help and I doubt we will," protested one youth.

"We can't leave our women and children alone in Vinland to sail back here later. Besides it would take four voyages to do that. And those back in Vinland would be without a ship," argued Magnus, pouting and protesting at the very thought of such an action.

"What if we take thirty men and they can build a ship with our help and we take ten children?" suggested Noddad.

"If they stayed with Inuit in igloos they could easily survive another winter. We were warm last winter in the igloos. And we should take the children from the Lysu Fiord as they have been most friendly too us," endorsed Magus.

"White Cloud told me the Inuit on the coast don't normally build igloos, but the winter coming up was so cold they did. I want us to take Olaf. We can draw lots for the rest. What say you men to Naddod's idea?" asked Thorfinn, looking for a vote on the matter.

They took their time to consider the proposal and then voted in favor of Naddod's idea.

Thorfinn longed to save everyone in the Settlement, but the ship was just too small. The ship could now hold only about another forty people. The Christians would have to learn to live with the Inuit for a winter or maybe two.

Eric had been living with Inuit since 1327 and he was doing fine, until his Inuit wife died and he went mad. Igloos were remarkably warm. And it was a joy not to have smelly animals sharing your accommodation. White Cloud was pleased to have Thorfinn's people too, as the people in Kangersuneq Fiord were hostile to the Inuit, and here in the Itivdlek Fiord he and his tribe could set up camp, under the shelter of Thorfinn and his men.

Thorfinn spotted a boat sailing by with all the speed it could manage. He guessed the shipwreck had been seen, and the news was being carried to Sandnes farm.

The boat sped into the Lysu Fiord screaming the news that Thorfinn had a ship.

The headmen Orm called for a gathering at Sandnes farm, but only the men from the Lysu Fiord attended the gathering. The people in Kangersuneq Fiord ignored the request. They told Eric the Hermit that they intended to wait until the ship was repaired before they would make any decisions. Prayers had been made to the Saints to intercede , and for ship to come and save them.

The men who did attend the gathering at Sandnes farm were grim faced and solemn. Many cursed Thorfinn's luck at having the ship washed up, where he lived. All of them wanted the ship to sail to Iceland. Vinland was full of thousands of Skraeling. In Iceland they could be with own people, and speak their own language. It would require a great change in their life styles to live in Vinland, and that change was unacceptable. Only Orm's pronouncement that the ship was unworthy to make the voyage round the deadly Cape Farewell swung the vote round to staying temporarily in Vinland and building a stronger ship to take them to Iceland later.

Orm omitted the one deciding factor—Thorfinn and his men were the best hunters and fighters in the Settlement, except for Eric the Hermit. They would kill anyone who attempted to take their ship, and it was their ship. Orm began to wonder what Europe was really like. The Settlement hadn't had any news of the outside world for sixteen years. Wars had broken out in less time than that in the past. Iceland couldn't be much warmer than Greenland. Would they be welcome there? His son Halfdan would love the chance to train to be an insipid priest, which could only be accomplished in

Iceland. A priest was not the path he wanted for his son.

Astrid walked into the great hall causing the men to almost jump from their seats at a young unmarried girl, daring to show herself at a men's gathering, when important discussion was being held.

"There is no need to worry a ship is coming and will arrive soon," she informed in a firm voice.

Orm jumped from his seat, his face red with anger and he bellowed loudly, "Go and live with your mad cousins for you are as mad as they. Go!"

Astrid was too proud to seek Orm's pardon and marched haughtily out the door, slamming it behind her. She would go and live with her cousins where she would be free to talk about her warm- island. Astrid walked passed Freda without speaking a word, to where the boat lay on the stony shoreline and rowed away.

Eric's kayak slid up to the shoreline, he smiled at Freda and remembered 1327.

"Is that Astrid? Where is she going?" he asked.

"Going to live with her mad cousins. Orm had her thrown out. He's sick of hearing about her 'warm-island'. We all are."

"Freda, Astrid is the daughter of Ingrid the Wise. Her eyes see what you do not. However, I will go and tell Noddad the good news. He can go and rescue his love from her cousins. Who is the boy by the water gathering driftwood?"

"My son Olaf. I forgot you don't know him, Eric. Come back to your own people Eric."

"I left my own people a year ago. I left the Norse sixteen years ago."

Eric yearned to know love and security, and his stay among the Norse had convinced him that if he was to grasp that love and security, he had to return to the Inuit. These Norse fools who wished to live like their ancestors were just too mad for his liking. Astrid could be more sane that them. Eric remembered the demonstration of Christian charity in 1327 which he had conveyed him to the Inuit world. It would be a warm winter in Greenland before the Inuit turned to Halfdan's God, and a church that perceived it to be the holder and giver of salvation. Halfdan was talking to the wind when he spoke to White Cloud and Fresh Water about Christianity. Eric chuckled at the thought of Inuit converting to that ridiculous religion. Thorfinn's religion wasn't quite as stupid, but not by much to Eric's way of thinking.

"Goodbye, Freda. I will not be meeting you again. I am returning to my people—the Inuit."

Eric experienced a great load of grief being lifted from his mind as strolled back to his kayak. He was free at last of the Norse civilization and all its trimmings. But before he returned to his own people, he had better take his kayak over land and visit Thorfinn and the Kangersuneq Fiord to and try and make the people see that the way forward was to join the Inuit. He would make one last effort to save the fools. Noddad also needed to be told about Astrid and how she had been thrown out.

Eric's eye sockets were deeper than those of most men. He had red hair, blue eyes, and large ears. He had to admit that even the Inuit couldn't see or hear as well as he could. But he conceded that Ingrid was the only person who could see ahead.

"Ingrid, is Noddad your choice for Astrid?" he asked aloud as he paddled along the fiord.

A resounding no echoed in Eric's head. Einar of the Orkneys shot into Eric's mind.

Eric heaped ridicule upon himself. It was clear he was not in touch with Ingrid's spirit as there no one like Einar of Orkneys living. Thorfinn was the nearest to man to Einar of Orkneys, but he had yet to face an open sea and conduct real warfare.

Eric focused his mind on the clear calm water in order to steer his mind away from such silly thoughts. He was unsuccessful, the message returned. A man like Einar of the Orkneys was Ingrid's choice of husband for her daughter Astrid. Eric was dazed, even someone like Orm the Bold wasn't good enough. Einar had been warrior but he was also rich and powerful. How was Astrid going to find a husband like that?

The entrance of the Itivdlek Fiord was the home of Astrid's cousins, Svein and Ingolf. Both of them pouted as they looked at their sickly animals, and then they gazed at their one room turf stone house.

"I don't want to live like this. It might have been fine for father, but not for us. And I don't want Thorfinn's Vinland. I want Astrid's island. We can get there. Row a boat to the East Settlement, from there to Iceland, and onto some island off Scotland. Then go fighting. War is for us. Not this. You gain plenty of loot in war and then live well on a farm with others doing all the work," said Svein impressed with his own idea.

"I agree. We could make that Thorfinn take us to the East Settlement first before he goes off to his wonderful Vinland, if he offered Astrid to his brother. She has to be of some use. Why not sell her so we can get to the East Settlement. It'll save us rowing," Ingolf said, his face brightened with excitement.

"She doesn't like him, Ingolf."

"Svein, who cares what she likes? Women marry where they are told. Astrid will marry Noddad," Ingolf gaped and bared his teeth at his brother for even bothering to consider Astrid. She wasn't blood kin. Ingrid's sister had married their father after they were born and she was found dead later.

"You are right Ingolf who cares, if she don't want him! It is what we want that matters. And we want Scotland. It is funny. She dreams of a 'warm-island' with castles, and it is us that are going to be living there while she rots in Vinland with Noddad. No books, no markets, and no pretty buildings for her to look at. Just plenty of Skraeling trying to kill her. Maybe one will take her for a slave. We will think of her while we drink ale in a tavern," the thought made him jeer with laughter as he leaned back on his heels.

"It truly is a good jest Astrid—she is so mad. Just so mad," declared Svein. Then he made a drawn out low howl. He saw Inuit children on the shoreline. His eyes held a look of utter bliss.

"Look what has come to call brother!

"Ooh and they be all alone. We could drown them but that is a bit quick. Why not burn the little savages?" Svein said with relish.

"That sounds so good. We chuck them and watch…"

Ingolf's mouth opened to speak, but then he appeared crestfallen. Svein wondered what was wrong.

"Look kayaks. We cannot have our fun. But we will get one of them Skraeling before we leave," whined Ingolf in sadistic glee.

"Oh and look who is sailing to Thorfinn's place? Halfdan the preacher-man. He is another one I would like to throw on a fire. He's always talking about hellfire. I could give him a good taste of it," Ingolf sniggered, congratulating himself, on thinking up such a clever joke.

'We will find plenty of creatures just like him in Scotland. There we will be free to rob, pillage, and rape it is going to be a grand life; it makes me feel good just to think about it. No more animals, hunting, or fishing—just plenty of real easy times ahead, brother."

"I'll get the whip out in case Astrid needs some gentle persuasion," assured Ingolf.

"How are we going to get to her come here? She does live at Sandnes farm and the men there are such pests." Svein grunted. The men of the West Settlement sickened him with their Norse code of honour, sharing, and looking after anyone who had fallen on hard times. What a boring life it was in the West Settlement. He thought about going to visit Thorfinn, but the thought of hearing bleating Halfdan made him decide to stay away. He would issue Thorfinn with his ultimatum later, after they had kidnapped Astrid.

"Look a boat is rowing towards us, Astrid is in the boat! Ooh now we can have fun. We don't have to kidnap her. Ooh this is so… good Ingolf!"

Astrid jumped out of the boat and marched up the slope to where her cousins stood, gaping with wild merry eyes at their victim strolling so calmly towards them.

"I have left Sandnes farm and wish to live here," said Astrid.

"You are our cousin by marriage and are most welcome, Astrid," said Ingolf. Astrid was unaware of the impending danger.

"Thorfinn has found a shipwreck and is repairing the ship." said Svein lazily.

"Wait cousins—a better ship than that is on its way," said Astrid lightly gazing out across the fiord.

"The one going to a warm-island with castles?" inquired Ingolf with raised eyebrows and voice touched with a mocking tone.

"Yes I feel that it is near and it will take me and you....no not you..."

The straggled words spoken by Astrid had no effect on the men. They chuckled at her with wild eyes. Astrid was blind to her peril. The men walked off and left Astrid to gather driftwood. Astrid thought about Thorfinn's ship and wondered how long it would take the men to repair it.

*****

Logs were hauled down the slope in readiness to be cut and to repair the three damaged planks. Men sang as they worked. They were so busy they didn't notice a group of people.

While Thorfinn and the working crew carried on a party of twenty three people were hurrying towards his farm. They reached the beach where Thorfinn and his men were working.

"We are from Pisigsarfix Fiord, we would like to go to Vinland?" asked the eldest man among who was twenty five.

Thorfinn counted six men, thirteen children and four women.

"You are more than welcome, but my men have said?"

"They are welcome very welcome!" shouted the men as they looked up from their work.

With six more men the work would be finished in days. The six women who lived in the Itivdlek Fiord rushed down the slope to greet the other women.

"We are making the sail and cooking the seal meat. We could do with extra hands," said Thorfinn's wife hoping she could get a few offers.

"That is what we are here for. Not to freeload. The children can help gather driftwood and the girls can help sew," replied the eldest of the women who was twenty seven.

Everyone was excited at the prospect of leaving as soon as possible.

Men craved into the wooden logs with axes. Women sew patches of skin to make a sail. Children combed the shoreline for driftwood to make tar, in order to seal the ship planks.

"Thorfinn don't you get inviting Astrid's mad cousins along," mocked one man.

"Went fishing them with once. And once was too often. I lost all me catch. They wanted to go a hunt down a polar bear and the polar bear decided to hunt them. I had to save them. And then the bear ate my fish," moaned one man.

"You should have done the Settlement a great service and not robbed the bear of his dinner," jeered Thorfinn, he wouldn't have saved any relation of Grimar. It was a happy day in the Settlement when Grimar sailed away.

Thorfinn forgot about Grimar's mad kin, and looked down at the beautiful coat on the logs and the yellow brown wood within the coat. Thorfinn sighed as he tried to vision the type of tree that produced such wood. There were thousands of the trees in Vinland. And no polar bears. He wouldn't be missing them. And most of all he wouldn't miss an ice floe.

"I wonder what the trees look like that have this kind of wood," pondered Noddad.

"I was just thinking that," answered Thorfinn marveling at the touch of the wood.

"None of us have ever seen a tree, so we don't know. There will be sights in Vinland to make our eyes pop," said one man helping to carry a log to the ship wreck.

"Don't forget there will be no King and Church coming to rob there. I won't miss them and I do remember them," snarled one man as he placed the log on the ground.

"Yes our grain will be all ours. Hadn't heard from the King in years. Naddod's axe would look well dressing the royal head or that of a bishop," shouted Magnus happily.

Thorfinn tried to hold back his laughter, but it was too hard he joined the men in ridicule of the King and church.

"I am not wasting my good axe on that unworthy maggot," remarked Noddad.

More laughter erupted from the men. These were goods days, working together for the greater goal of leaving Greenland. One man thought of his only child, a boy of nine. He was going to get the chance to grow up in a land of plenty and warmth far away from the greedy Church and King. If they went to Iceland they would have to pay the King and the Church to live in poverty. The Church and the King were just as dangerous as the Skraeling. Leif Ericson had brought that religion to Greenland, which explained why he didn't get on too well with the Skraeling in Vinland.

"What happens when the ships of Europe reach the shores of Vinland?" asked a youth.

It was a question no one had thought of. Yet they knew it would happen. Noddad was the first to offer a forecast.

'With the way the seas are at the moment it will many long years away. And I think men will rise against the abuse of Mother Church by then. And they will find our children waiting for them," said Noddad.

"Noddad is right. It has been sixteen years and we haven't seen a ship. One hundred and sixteen years before they get to Vinland. That is what I say," shouted one man as he helped put down the last of the logs.

Thorfinn thought the prediction may well be true. It would be that long before a European walked on the shores of Vinland. And then they would have to be able to stay.

Thorfinn was thinking of Vinland, when Eric the Hermit paddled up towards the shoreline in his kayak. Eric paddled the kayak with same swift ease of the Inuit, only his red hair and blue eyes marked him out as different from the Inuit. He had lived with them since 1327 and only came back here last summer. Eric was a hermit and an outcast. Thorfinn, although he could mix with the Inuit, didn't think like them the way Eric did. Eric had ceased to be Norse in 1327. He was able to see things Norsemen couldn't see or hear. Thorfinn felt uneasy with the man. So did his companions.

The enterprise of repairing a shipwreck had Eric's eyes staring. They had all gone daft. Straining their backs and arms so much so that they had to strip down to their waists, because they were so hot, in spite of the cold breeze whisking across the fiord. What reason was there to journey to a land known only to them, from dubious sagas? Vinland was inhabited by highly violent natives who had sent the Vikings running for their long ships. And, of course the fools first had to survive a four hundred mile voyage in the open sea to reach this fabled land. Vinland was known to his Inuit people. As boy growing up with them he had heard of the odd encounter between Inuit and Vinland Skraeling, but the tales didn't encourage him to put his feet on Vinland for the sake of mere sunshine. It was the country's only attraction. Greenland had plenty of food. Igloos were warm and comfortable. Norse houses stank because farm animals were kept inside. The high death toll in the West Settlement was due to that ridiculous practice. Eating the animals and not keeping them would eradicate the problem.

There were seals, fish, foxes, bears, and birds in Greenland, so it was folly to keep animals that caused sickness. Norse customs in Greenland was folly to the highest degree. In a crisp voice full of mockery Eric declared, "Thor I am not going to go to Vinland. Greenland is my home and with the Inuit I will stay. And I challenge you great Thor to decree otherwise," he flicking his hand sharply into the air.

Eric chuckled at his own joke. He leaned back, and gazed at a cloud, and continued to mock Thor.

"You are about as powerful as Christ!"

Eric was so amused he almost leaned back too far and nearly lost control of the kayak. But Eric hadn't mislaid his black humor when he slid the kayak up onto the shoreline, where the men were still hard at work. Thorfinn's sweaty fair hair and chest didn't quell Eric's chuckling, it just made it worst.

Thorfinn gritted his teeth and glared at Eric, he knew that him and his men were the source of Eric's humor.

"I'm glad we have brought a smile to your sour face, Eric the Hermit," snarled Thorfinn pronouncing Eric's name and status with venom.

Eric stood with his legs apart and his hand's on his hips, Eric's humor was gone. Eric the Inuit spoke from his head not from his heart.

"Greenland has plenty. The Skraeling in Vinland will kill you. Do you hot head Norse think you can do what the Inuit cannot? The voyage is an unnecessary risk. One that need not be taken," lectured Eric.

"You are more Inuit than the Inuit. I don't know why you came back to the Norse settlement, Eric."

"Madness from sorrow I suppose," replied Eric honestly.

Without pity Thorfinn lashed out at the man he regarded as a lowly outcast. Thorfinn snarled in rage.

"You lost a wife. Men have lost wives. Not one woman with child survived last winter and every child under eight are dead. I weep for them. Not for you."

Eric felt his chest had been punched in. The death of his Inuit wife still ate at his heart. He left the Inuit because they too wished him to forget her, which drove him to return to the Nose community. Norse folly was sending him back to where he belonged, with the Inuit.

"None of your children died because you stayed in igloos that White Cloud built for you."

"We don't have any children under seven and five men here don't have wives...My brother doesn't have one."

Eric cunningly threw the conversation on to a new topic.

"Astrid had been thrown of Orm's house," he injected.

The news about Astrid's eviction made Noddad put down his axe and stop chopping at a log. His eyes stretched along with his mouth. Noddad breathing was heavy from worry.

"What! Why?" he demanded as he grabbed Eric's shoulder.

Eric took no offence; it was the reaction he had expected.

"She rattled on to Orm about going to that warm island again, Astrid has gone to live with her cousins."

"They are mad!" snapped Noddad in alarm at Astrid's plight.

Eric was moved by Naddod's display of his love for Astrid, even hough he considered the pair incompatible. Astrid was Ingrid's daughter, and Ingrid would never have married Noddad. Plus the fact that he had odd notion that Ingrid really did want someone like Einar of the Orkneys, and Noddad wasn't that kind of man.

He did feel the need to assure Noddad that Astrid would be safe however.

"She can leave and will. You are the nearest neighbour where else could or would she go?"

Eric's calm confidence and plausible tone caused Noddad to settle down. His panic subsided. But he wasn't prepared to tolerate anymore of Astrid's silly ideas. She was going to Vinland with him.

"Thorfinn, why not stay here?" Eric tried to instill reason once more.

Thorfinn became very serious. His eyes grew cold as he answered.

"You can't be Inuit. And you never will be Eric. No matter how you try. Even if marry another Inuit woman."

Thorfinn held Eric's gaze as he uttered his emotionless prediction of Eric's miserable future.

"You will walk in two worlds for all the days of your life Eric."

It was a future Eric was totally unprepared for and one he wished to avoid. The Inuit ways of life pulled hard at his heart strings. European religion and culture would evaporate his mental stability. He would rather face a polar bear attack then be plunged into such a world. Eric sought to end the slander of his Inuit life. He turned his back on them, and hoped to turn his back on their way of life. He would take his kayak up the Godthaab Fiord, and there he would spend some time in solitude before asking White

Cloud to take him back into the tribe.

"I can only take twenty four extra passengers, if they want to build a ship in Vinland and sail back to the old world they can do so. This ship can't make it round Cape Farewell. Can you take this message round the settlement for me Eric?" asked Thorfinn to Eric's retreating back.

Eric swung round, and with a sombre voice embedded with patience he replied.

"I can and will. But again I say, Thorfinn—why not stay here. You know the Inuit ways. In Vinland you will not be able to stay Norse any more than you can here. So why go? And the devoted Christians in the Kangersuneq Fiord may try and take this ship by force. They are much more attached to the homelands. They long to live in Iceland even though they have never seen it and known of the famines and feuds the place has—not forgetting the earthquakes and eruptions."

Thorfinn was sadly and grimly aware the Eric's evaluation of the mentality of the folk living around the Kangersuneq Fiord was only too accurate. They welcomed a visit from Bible bashing Halfdan and no one living in the other fiords did, even though they adhered to the Christian faith. Trouble was definitely a strong possibility with those folk. The presence of White Cloud's tribe at the edge of the fiord may not be enough to keep that bunch of Norse Christians from trying to steal the ship; guards would have to be placed.

Eric's grin suggested he had some more information to give.

Thorfinn's eyes froze as he pondered the disastrous message Eric was about to proclaim.

"Young Halfdan is heading this way. I must be leaving to deliver your important message. While he tries to save your souls from the Christian hell," chuckled Eric, his body shaking with laughter.

Repulsive chatter about the Bible—right when they had wood to chop wasn't going to be tolerated. Halfdan's incessant preaching was a nightmare. The only trouble was a man could wake up from a nightmare; such escape wasn't possible from Halfdan's voice. Eric heard Thorfinn's cursing all the way back to his kayak.

"Halfdan—if he wasn't the headman's son and a friend of White Cloud I would throw him in the fiord! I blame my cousin Freda for teaching him to read. We wouldn't have had this trouble, if he hadn't have been able to read the darn book of Saints! If I ever find that book, I will chuck it in the sea!"

Out on the water Eric ridiculed the Norse Gods in a fit of wild humor.

"Your followers sure are dim wits Thor! " Eric laughed away to himself as his paddle plunged into the water. The names of Astrid and Halfdan pieced through his mockery of Thor though.

"Astrid maybe? But Halfdan—I can't imagine him doing anything excepting giving people ear ache! And neither of them follow Thor!"

Eric opted to drag the kayak overland rather than take the longer route round by sea to reach the Kangersuneq Fiord. He smiled as he thought about how easy the task was. The vessels of the Norse were far too heavy and clumsy to be dragged over even a short patch of terrain. But Eric's hilarity resumed as he thought of Thorfinn working hard away.

***

Men poured in sweat under Greenland's feeble summer light cutting the pine logs. Women wove a sail with every kind of fabric they could find. Children gathered driftwood to make pitch. It was all they had to seal the ship with. Thorfinn placed a guard around their valuable gift from Thor. It was a sad day in the settlement when they to fight off other Norse living here. Norse customs of sharing and caring were dying like Greenland itself.

The flurry of work was interrupted by the arrival of the headman's son sixteen year old Halfdan, with his usual cheery vibrant mood. He was noted to be slow to anger, fearless, and loyal friend. But he preached the Bible with more fury than any priest. Sneers quickly appeared on the workers' faces, a warning growl came from their throats at his approach.

"I have come to bless the ship. Fresh Water saw it wash up on the shoreline. Everyone knows about it. And I can read a passage from the book of Saints," offered Halfdan hoping to convert the Viking enclave of the West Settlement to Christianity.

Thorfinn's axe was in mid-air and his nostrils flared. It was hard for him to curb his anger against the Christian youth whose sole intent in life was to preach Christianity—a ridiculous religion as far as he and his people were concerned. But Halfdan was Orm's son and a friend of White Cloud, so Thorfinn took a deep breath before speaking.

"No." That one plainly spoken word wiped away all of Halfdan's cheer. He guessed his faith was going to be attacked and he quickly mounted a defense for his faith.

"Vikings made human sacrifices to Odin and Thor," pointed out Halfdan in accusation against the Norse religion. Halfdan was prepared to commit himself, to fight for Mother Church. Let Thorfinn see if he can win that argument, thought Halfdan.

"Yes the Gods didn't want them and were insulted, which is why we got Christians as punishment," hissed Thorfinn between his teeth, his gleaming axe still in mid-air. Thorfinn's answer had anyone chuckling except Halfdan who pushed back his blonde hair, annoyed that he had failed to find a good response to Thorfinn's attack on his faith. Perhaps he should try and convert the Inuit. Fresh Water and White Cloud never abused his faith, they could well be on the verge of converting, and more worthy of his efforts than Thorfinn.

"Hmmn. I will go and preach to White Cloud and his tribe. They are just at the edge of the fiord right now. I will be welcomed there."

"Only because you saved little Shining Rock from a polar bear. And only White Cloud and Fresh Water can understand the Norse language so there is no point in you going to barking to the Inuit with Christianity. Your church hates the Inuit. It won't even allow trade with them."

Sunlight hit Thorfinn's blade and it shone into Halfdan's eyes making them flicker. Thorfinn thought he made the boy wince and felt ashamed. Halfdan was the very youth he wanted to come to Vinland with him.

"Why don't forget joining the church and come with us to Vinland, Halfdan?"

Vinland. A land without books. The very notion tore at Halfdan's heart. Hunting, fishing, and fighting were not for him. He longed to be a clerk, preach the true word of God, and to see the church return to basics of the scriptures. The church had lost its way—otherwise the events in 1327 wouldn't have happened. A revival was what was needed and he yearned to be a part of that revival. To spend his days studying the Bible, going out among the poor and serving the poor, as Christ had done. Writing with real ink was something he looked forward to doing. Vinland offered him nothing.

"I plan on going to Iceland and join the church. She has lost her way like Astrid and needs to be shown the right path to take." Halfdan turned his back on Thorfinn and went back to his boat to sail off to visit White Cloud's tribe. Halfdan gave up trying to save Thorfinn's soul, then swung round to face Thorfinn.

"You might want to look at this map," advised Halfdan. He waved a map of Vinland under Thorfinn's nose.

Thorfinn dignity spiraled. Halfdan was clever. Much more clever than himself. Thor wouldn't be too pleased by him running Halfdan down. Why did the youth have to be Christian, and a dreadfully annoying one at that?

"I will leave you with the map and drawings, while I go and spread God's word," exclaimed Halfdan.

As Halfdan retreated toward the water and climbed into his boat, Thorfinn felt pangs of pity for his Inuit friends.

Halfdan pulled back hard on the oars as he made a massive effort to spread the Christian message.

***

White Cloud and his younger brother Fresh Water caught sight of Halfdan paddling towards their camp site.

"Halfdan comes to tells more tales about his angry God I think, Fresh Water."

"I think so too. I will take him hunting. That way your ears will be spared. I don't understand this God. Halfdan is above other men among the Norse. His God is his only failing. I think he is more clever than your friend Thorfinn," implied Fresh Water.

"Halfdan mind is sharp and his courage high. I wish he and Thorfinn would join our people and stay here. I am glad Eric is coming back to us. He mourned too long for his wife. There is much food and plenty to keep them warm. Why must they think of going on a dangerous voyage to a land filled with warriors that would show the men no mercy, and take their women and children? The ways of the Norse are strange to me Fresh Water. Eric is different but he lived with as boy. Only went back to his people when his wife died. I suppose that is why he is different."

His young brother shook his head. He would try once more to persuade Halfdan to stay and join the tribe. The stories Halfdan had told him of the lands to the east sounded terrible, and every Inuit knew what the people in the west were like, they had seen their people killed by them. The Kangersuneq folk would kill any Inuit they could find, except the family living at the edge—they were friendly to the Inuit.

"Fresh Water, White Cloud greetings," said Halfdan cheerfully.

"I am going hunting come with me Halfdan," invited Fresh Water.

Halfdan considered the offer. He needed to be gone for a while in order for his father to recover and forget his outburst. A hunting trip with Fresh Water was always good and he needed quiet open spaces to plan out his life. He was thinking of taking a sailing boat to the East Settlement some 250 miles south, and from there seeking passage on a ship to Iceland. Or maybe even Norway and entering the church. The tale of 1327 came to mind and he needed to see that it never happened again. That could only be achieved by mass reform within the church. And to reform the church, he had to join the church. It was the most important task in Christendom. The whole fabric of society stood to be ripped asunder if the task wasn't accomplished.

"That would be good Fresh Water," answered Halfdan.

White Cloud cast a glance at the sky and thanked the spirits for influencing Halfdan and taking him away from the camp. Halfdan had saved his daughter Shining Rock, and he would never openly insult Halfdan, who considered his act of fighting off a polar bear as nothing. The youth was so different from the hated Norse people in Kangersuneq Fiord.

"Pointed Rocks is a good place let us good there, Fresh Water," uttered Halfdan, remembering that was where his father wished to meet him.

Fresh Water grabbed his harpoon and set off with Halfdan to Pointed Rocks, where his father was holding a meeting and he could catch up with him there.

THE SHIP

Out fishing at the edge of Godthaab Fiord on the north side of the Settlement two youths caught sight of a sailing ship. They had to blink twice.

"Can it be?" One asked the other hardly able to believe the glorious sight.

"It is...it is a ship! Put up the sail and row, row hard—get to the main settlement, we must tell everyone! Oh no! Look the Skraeling and our men are fighting. Errr...we had better go and tell everyone about the ship. They look as if they can handle the Skraeling."

In the Kangersuneq Fiord on the bleak stony shoreline, a group of women searched for driftwood. One woman of twenty four raised her head. Her eyes barely opened, her mouth was sagged. She was too tried to go on. The woman turned her head to look at her daughter further up the shoreline. A life of drudgery, with a good chance of dying in childbirth was what awaited her daughter in Greenland. She had been wicked to bring the child into this cold icy hell. The woman turned her head again to gaze at the calm green water that offered a solution to all her worries. In its depths she would find peace. She walked over the stony beach towards the water's edge. Tiny ripples washed over her feet and her ankles. The water rose over her body until it covered her. The women noticed what she was doing.

"No...no!" cried her friends in horror as they raced toward the water's edge. It was too late. The woman was beneath the water. All they could do was look on helplessly. The children couldn't grasp the woman's mental anguish that had led her to end her life, as they stood unable to move. Her body floated on the water.

"We have to make plans to leave Greenland. Thorfinn has a ship. Let us make those men of ours listen. We demand a gathering. We the women of Kangersuneq demand action! Not moaning and dreaming of trade that hasn't come for sixteen years!" yelled one woman.

Furious at the death of their friend, they began to march up the slope and to the church. One man heading towards a boat encountered the group.

"You man. We the women have had enough. We are going with Thorfinn and taking the children with us. You dreamy men can stay here and die of cold. But we are not," shouted one woman.

"We are leaving. We are leaving," chanted the women loudly.

The man was shaken, he could tell the women were in a violent mood, and no amount of talk was going to alter their course of action. He ran off to alert his male friends.

"The women are on the march. They say they are leaving with Thorfinn," declared the man, baffled and horrified.

The men, who had just returned from a fishing trip, stared at him unwilling to believe the women would react in such a manner. Until they saw the twenty five women swooping down the hill chanting and waving logs in the air.

"Ingrid drowned herself," screamed one of the women to the sixteen men.

Suicide struck a terrible blow in the hearts of the men. Ingrid had lost her husband and six children. It was understandable that she couldn't go on. And the women were right. This land wasn't worth one life. It was too cold, too dark, and there was nothing here but fish and game. If they stayed then and their children would die.

"We should call a gathering and make plans to leave," shouted one of the men.

The women stopped their march half way down the slope. Hope planted its deceit in the women's hearts. It was slight, but enough to turn the tide of despair. The women formed a circle and began to chat among themselves.

"The ship mightn't be big enough to take all of us. But the first trip should be for the children. Being only small and weighing less the whole lot could go out on the first trip," reasoned one woman looking for support among her female friends.

There was rapid response of nodding heads, with grim faces to match. The thought of their children living in warmer land eased the pain they experienced over the loss of their friend. The woman's child would live in a warmer and safer land.

The men with the fishing boat full of fish emptied their catch on the shoreline and hurried back to the boat. They rowed upstream to spread the word. A gathering was being called to arrange leaving Greenland. Farm after farm received the message and entire families packed up, going to the central church for the meeting. Boats arrived at the shoreline of the church. Glum faced men embarked from the boats, leaving the women and children down on the shoreline, while they went to discuss the important business of leaving Greenland. Sixty men trudged to the church at the top of the rise. No man spoke or offered a greeting.

The oldest man who was twenty nine took his place in front of the altar. He waited for all the men to arrive and the door was shut.

"Men, we are here to discuss Thorfinn's plan to go to Vinland. There are many here and in the rest of the Settlement who think we should go to Iceland. Orm has seen the ship and sent the message that the ship is too small to make the voyage round Cape Farewell. But in Vinland we could build a ship strong enough to make a voyage to Iceland. The ship Thorfinn found is only a small ship that came here in 1327 and if he hadn't found good pine logs the ship would have been petty useless. The women want all the children in the settlement to go on the first voyage. I have given the facts, but I want to hear what each man has to say."

"The current to Vinland is less dangerous than that to Iceland. But what of the Skraeling? And remember Erik the Red's brood were driven back from the shores as it was indefensible. There are thousands of Skraeling. We couldn't fight them off," said one man, rejecting the idea as folly.

"We would have settled there years ago if it wasn't for the damn Skraeling. Thorfinn is friendly with the Skraeling here and thinks he can be friends with the Skraeling there. I say it is madness to think there can be peace with savages," objected another man with teeth showing and waving a fist.

"Our children would be killed by the Skraeling!" roared other men in violent agreement. The leader at the front was wishing some other man could conduct the meeting. He searched the church for calm faces which might indicate calm reasonable heads.

"The Skraeling in Vinland would kill us but not the children. Remember the sagas and the visit in 1294. The Skraeling take women and children to push up the tribe's numbers, but they kill the men. And we would only have to be there long enough to build a ship to take us to Iceland. We haven't got to stay there. "

The leader's quiet tone began to contain the fear and drunken rage in the men at the church.

"Let us vote men, before our women vote with the sticks they are carrying," jested the leader standing at the front with the altar at his back.

There was a round of laughter echoing inside the stone church. Cakes of dirt were crusted on every church item. Including the Bible chained to the wall. There were no educated people in the Kangersuneq Fiord to read the Bible, so no one opened it. Halfdan made a visit last summer and read passages from the book of Saints and gave sermons, which filled them with delight. The boy was the nearest thing they had to a priest. He even performed a marriage. But the couple and their baby died in the winter.

"Before we consider the facts let us recall, all the children under eight are dead along with all the pregnant women. We cannot stay. The East Settlement maybe safe at the present but they will soon fall too. And they wouldn't welcome us, they have lost the Norse traditions. The route to Iceland is far longer and more dangerous. There could well be some little island in Vinland where we could stay out the way of the Skraeling until we can build a better ship. There is also another possibility too that no one has voiced. We could stay in the north part of Vinland which is similar to Greenland, where the Skraeling don't live and just sail south a bit to collect the wood to build our ship and return to our homeland, where our hearts are," said the leader.

The third option sounded like harp music to the ears of the men. If Thorfinn wanted to live with violent Skraeling, he could go there after they had built the ship to take them home back to Norse lands.

"The last option is the best," injected one man.

Hands went up in favor of the third option. The leader nodded. He was so pleased not to have riot with the men and another one with the women outside.

One man at the back of the church sighed. The vote had failed to consider Thorfinn's consent. He wasn't a Christian; his fighting skill could have sent a Viking running, and there were more just like him. It was folly to think Thorfinn was going to stay where they wanted and allow them to command his ship. Thorfinn's first loyalty was to his people in the Itivdlek Fiord. Second came those in the Lysu Fiord, and last came those in the Kangersuneq Fiord. True, there were thirty eight men in the Kangersuneq Fiord and only eight fighting men in Itivdlek Fiord. Thorfinn might decide not engage in a fight and sail off without taking anyone and never coming back. His daughter would be left to die in Greenland. All because some greedy men wanted a ship they hadn't found or repaired. Anger detonated in the man, his voice was extraordinary loud as he bellowed.

"Thorfinn has to agree. Do you think he will?" The advice dispersed their votes to the air. Thorfinn was a legend—fearless loyal, hardworking, and man of honour—but stubborn.

"Do you plan to fight him?"

They knew there would be a great loss of life and most likely on their side. Thorfinn and his men were the best sailors and boat builders in the Settlement. None of them could equal Thorfinn in anything, except faith in Christ. No wreath of good deeds could buy a place on heaven without faith in Christ. Thorfinn's pagan faith was an insurmountable obstacle. The Lysu Fiord folk weren't as faithful to the church as the people in the Kangersuneq Fiord. They could always find some accommodation with Thorfinn's pagan faith.

"I have another proposal. We stay in the northern areas away from the violent Skraeling and Thorfinn delivers us timber to make our ship and sail home," injected the leader.

The men debated all the difficulties and rewards of the proposals. The last proposal seemed to be the best one. Thorfinn was unlikely to refuse them a load of timber. He was too proud to rebuff such a mild request.

The leader at the front of the altar longed to reach a decision, before the men opted to use their fists.

Out the church women exchanged looks of impatient anger.

"What is there to discuss?" snapped one women.

"Nothing. But men dither and debate, then they charge into something without thinking," chimed in another woman waving her broken branch of thin driftwood back and forth in growing rage.

One of the younger men at the back of the gathering opened the church door just wide enough, to see the angry mob of women.

"Men, our women look ready for war!" he warned.

"Err…" whined the leader at the front.

"All in favor of the last idea?" shouted the leader hastily.

Every hand flew up. The leader sighed with relief. Angry women folk were worse than Thorfinn in their opinion.

The men all smiled pleased with themselves and stroll haughtily out of the church. The men boldly announced their decision and looked for praise and approval. The women informed them that they had no intention of exchanging one icy hell for another icy hell, and ordered them back into the church and to come out only after a decent resolution had been reached.

Subdued and sheepishly the men returned to the church. They

had reached the door when youths who had been out fishing raced up to the church, yelling at the top of their lungs.

"A ship, flying the Royal standard is sailing up the fiord!"

The news instantly swept away the last proposal. The crowd of sixty two adults froze, then breathed rapidly, their mouths open and lost for words. The object of all their hope and desire was sailing towards them. God in his mercy had heard an answered their prayers. Their King and Church hadn't forgotten them. The episode in 1327 didn't even enter into their thinking.

"Good thing we called a gathering. Everyone is here to welcome the ship and hear the news," uttered the leader of the group of men.

Everyone smiled, nodded, and made murmurs of agreement. Children cheered and jumped up and down. Excitement exploded among the people of Kangersuneq Fiord.

Eric had just arrived at the fiord and overheard the joyous commotion.

Fools to the highest degree was what the Kangersuneq Fiord folk were. Only sixteen years ago they had cheered at a Royal ship and now they gave a repeat performance of their lunacy. Eric had no plan to greet any men on the Royal ship.

He intended to spy on it. He walked briskly along the high ground. There was nice group of bushes and a hole to hide in which over looked the church where they were sure to hold their welcoming party for the ship. The people in the Kangersuneq Fiord were the most Christian Norse in the Settlement and always talking of life in Norway. A land they had never seen, but pulled hard at the core of their spirits. Sadly the Kangersuneq Fiord was the hardest last winter. Only eighteen children had survived. The grief had caused a type of madness in the community. He shook his head as he waited for the ship make its progress along the Kangersuneq Fiord.

Eric's Kayak was down on the water edge, left in a tiny cove. If the ship proved to be bad news, he could paddle unnoticed in his kayak and then overland to the Itivdlek Fiord and to alert Thorfinn about the ship. Thorfinn was a man of action and he had never forgiven the King. If the ship was out to commit robbery like in 1327, Thorfinn and his men were more than capable of ending any plots the Royal ship was hatching.

Eric went unnoticed by the thrilled assemble gathered at the wharf to greet the ship. Eric decided it was senseless to wait for the ship as he had previously planned. It would take a long time before the ship arrived. High up on the hill he would be able to see it, meanwhile he could do a bit of hunting before he returned to his chosen hiding spot. The silly Kangersuneq Fiord folk would probably hold a feast to celebrate while they waited for the pirate ship to arrive. He had to admit that Thorfinn wasn't stupid enough to give the occupants of the Royal ship any food at all. In fact Eric could see a Viking raid taking place, if Thorfinn learnt of this ship's visit.

THE ATTACK

The church Emissary swallowed his panic. His legs wobbled with each sway of the wooden vessel. A cluster of gleaming blue green ice was blocking the ship's path. What he asked himself, if those ice floes expanded and blocked the way out altogether? This single square sailing vessel had been his prison. Since the beginning of the long hideous voyage, he had been worried about being imprisoned in Greenland. The Emissary wished the Bishop had not forced him to undertaken this voyage and mission. The Bishop had made it sound as if he was bestowing on him a wondrous assignment to the papal court, instead of a trip to ghastly Greenland.

The sailors seemed immune to the ship's rocking and could walk across the ever moving deck with ease. He was hit by sickness and constantly had to watch very step he took on the wet deck. The ship's movement, coupled with his intensified emotions, resulted in turmoil for the man. The Emissary had a burning impulse to terminate this assignment. The ice floes had ruined his illusions of religious grandeur.

The ship's Captain didn't care one fragment about his terrible discomfort. The man avoided him every time he tried to speak. When he did condescend to speak to him his manner was less than respectful. The Captain spoke to his crew and the English archers, but not with him. Only his companion Grimar showed any concern for his welfare.

Grimar had picked up on the Emissary floundering emotions. The pious prattling oaf could end the mission with a wave of his hand. He had to recuperate the mission. He had spent sixteen years waiting and planning. He couldn't have it tossed aside because a few ice floes conjured up terror in the Emissary.

Grimar approached the Emissary. He secretly despised the man. The Emissary was a thin man and far too young to be entrusted with any mission. Especially this one which was Grimar's mission of revenge. His chief target was Thorfinn and his family. If the man had any family he would kill them slowly, while Thorfinn watched. The torment on Thorfinn's face, the rage that would engulf him at not being able to save his family. Revenge like that would at last silence the chaos in his head.

Grimar cast an eye over the English archers were they really as deadly as he had been told? Certainly they had arms like he had never seen before; their arms resembled knotted tree branches. The bows they carried stood at six feet high. It would take an awful amount of strength to pull the draw string. So it was doubtful whether the crude bow could send an arrow very far. Which could well mean some of his tormentors may escape. The stupid Emissary shouldn't have listened to that other priest in England, telling him how great these archers were. The priest was English, like the archers, of course he would praise up his countrymen. Encouraging and pampering the Emissary was challenging work. Descending into the role of a zealous religious companion, Grimar softly navigated the sliding deck with easy, and came up alongside the dithering Emissary.

"Emissary, we are entering the fiords and will soon walk on dry land. I know the Saints are with us on this voyage. I can feel their presence."

Grimar's pious expression gave the Emissary renewed faith. Grimar was truly a man of God. He should give due consideration to entering the church, rather than thinking he was unworthy to be a man of God. The men on this ship didn't have the humble faith that was buried in Grimar's soul.

"Grimar this proves that God means you to be a priest. I beg you to think again. A fisherman in England? You don't speak the language and I don't think God intends for you to be a fisherman."

"I will think on it. Perhaps you are right. But it could be that the Saints are guiding us because of our holy mission Emissary."

The Emissary considered Grimar's words. He could well be right. The ship's Captain had said this was the easiest voyage to Greenland in all its history. Clearly God was parting the ice and calming the sea, just as he had done for Moses.

An ice floe to the right of the ship made his faith plummet. The accursed thing seem to be following the ship, waiting to crash into the side and rip a hole in it, taking him into the freezing waters below. This land belonged to Satan. The Emissary gazed over to the ship's Captain with his eyes on the sea.

The ship's Captain was consumed with hatred at the sight of the ice. He steered the ship past each ice floe. Arctic white lay across Greenland which rushed head-long to the sea. The coastline was a graveyard for ships.

He forgot his misery, noted the concern on the faces of his crew, and sought to lift their spirits.

"So this is Greenland. Can anyone see much Green?" shouted the Captain in both Norse and English for the benefit of the English archers on board. He hoped his jest would relieve the strain on his crew and the archers, due to the sight of the towering ice floes. Raw dark snorts of laughter echoed around the deck. The captain knew he had succeeded.

"Keep an eye on our friend to the right, it seems to want to accompany is into the fiord, but it is a very unwelcome guest," the Captain jested in black humor.

The thin church Emissary was dumbfounded that the Captain could jest over ice floes alongside the ship. The man was clearly mad. A crazed fool was steering the ship. He prayed to the Saints to preserve him from fools.

"Never fear Emissary, the fiord is just ahead," assured the ship's Captain sensing his important passenger was about to have a panic attack.

Panic subsided slightly. Just a little while longer then the ice floes would be in retreat. He would be in a fiord, like the fiords of his home in Norway. A barrier of waves sealed the path to the West Settlement.

The Captain had to wait for a benevolent intermission by the sea before conducting the final phase of the voyage. The sky cleared, the wind dropped, and a calm channel gave the Captain the opportunity he required.

The ice that petrified the Emissary slipped back. The Emissary began thanking a list of Saint's for their intercession with the Lord God. The Captain began to think of the ice floes and cold blue light, that shook his soul. It was time to retire from long voyages, and live in a warmer land.

"St. Christopher we give thanks and praise," wailed the Emissary.

"Never heard for that saint," remarked a sailor, pulling rope.

"St. Christopher—the Saint for travelers," protested the Emissary. A common sailor had spoken to him without being spoken to first. He was representing Mother Church.

"Is he now?" uttered the youth rather disinterested as his mind turned back to the ropes.

Shoddy ill-manner sailors were crude and vulgar. The English Archers didn't speak Norse but they seemed to have the same ring to their voices as the rowdy sailors. The archers were most likely reliving tales of rape, pillage and raiding the French and Scottish people. Still he needed the killers. His fellow priest in England had assured him that they would be very skilled in their work and a priest didn't lie to another priest. He had purchased the required equipment necessary for their task.

It was the ship's Captain that concerned him. He was stupid and he couldn't even see how dangerous the ice floes were. Would he be able to see the dangerous devils that lurked in the West Settlement? The Emissary glanced over at Peter the English archer. He approved of the man. He realized the danger the ship was in.

The English archer Peter wasn't engaged in reckless laughter, he was getting set to read the terrain of an unknown land.

Peter, whose eyes had been schooled in the forests and mountains of England, surveyed the land. Most men looked at a forest. His vision stripped the forest of its trees and focused on the undergrowth. His ear was tuned to the clatter of rabbit's feet. Peter often took a trail that even deer would avoid. A man seeking to hide by walking in a stream stood no chance of evading Peter. His skills had saved the life of Lord Percy's steward and an entire village during a Scottish raid. Peter was a legend in the border land of North East England. In France he knew where the enemy was and simply avoided them. He now applied his talent to evaluate Greenland.

Greenland was a fortress minus battlements and towers, yet a more formidable deterrent to invasion or escape, due to its location and weather. Greenland's climate was a disaster, on the verge of bolting in all who failed to make a run of it. To Peter the land said, "go while you may, for those who linger will feel the fingers of death in Greenland."

Barking seals basking on the rocks seemed to be laughing at their foolish errand. Should he and his fellow archers have accepted such daft employment? It was the message given to him in church in England while he was praying, that led him to take on this strange employment far from home, with people who didn't speak English. St. Ann wouldn't be prayed to again if she did not deliver on her promise. He would find another Saint to pray to. There were plenty to select from.

"Ice, Mark. I never saw ice that high even in damn Scotland. Why did the priest want to come here anyway?"

"I don't know Peter, I didn't ask. The pay is very good," shrugged Mark as if it didn't matter. He didn't want his friend to know their real reason and hoped he wouldn't ask.

Mark's logic had failed. Peter was astonished. Mark had lived in a Lords' castle since he was seven. He knew the workings of the nobility and the church. Yet he hadn't thought to ask why this church Emissary from Norway wanted archers?

"You didn't ask you dim wit!" snapped Petered in disgust and was tempted to punch Mark for his outrageous folly. Mark snorted before he admitted the truth.

"An English priest caught Jack drinking the church wine for the mass and they had guards with them. They were going to hang Jack. Then that Norse sin-seller came out with his offer to spare Jack and give us good pay if we escorted him to Greenland. Being it was named Greenland, I kind of thought it would be green and fairly nice place. And come to think of it, you were keen for employment," accused Mark in a grumpy unforgiving manner.

Peter wiped the back of his hand over his mouth. The church snatched one tenth of everything a man had, leaving many a family short of food in the winter. But let a boy of fourteen take a sip of wine and out comes the noose. The priest where he lived had raped Peter's cousin. The poor lass lay on a pallet afterwards for a week. Peter recalled how the priest had merrily walking through the woods without a care. The priest cared plenty went an arrow entering his throat, and he drowned in his own blood.

"Sorry Mark of course you had to agree. Jack is one of us. But you should have told me."

Mark let off a bark of laughter.

"That Emissary and the English sin-seller would be dead if I had and we can't have you bringing an army of sin-sellers after us."

"True I would have. But what does the sin-seller want with ten archers Mark?" asked Peter in a nosy manner.

"He is a frightened rabbit that one, And the ship's Captain tells me the Greenland is inhabited by Skraeling. They are pagans that live by hunting and fishing. I think he wants us to protect him from them."

"Do he now," snarled Peter. There was no amusement in his tone of voice. "The creature that bothers me is Grimar. He acts one ways and thinks another. Reminds me of some knights. Only I think Grimar is worse than them Peter."

Mark was very puzzled by the foreboding feelings he had towards the Norseman from Greenland. Were all the people here like him? Mark had doubts about that, Grimar seemed a loner. He been in many battles and raids, but the character of this man was new to him. Mark was certain he had to be watched and kept within the reach of weapons. The sin-seller seemed be too fond of Grimar. Being haughty, arrogant, aloof, and humorless, the Emissary had shared qualities with Mark's former Lord. However the Emissary lacked his former Lord's self-restraint and astuteness. Grimar hadn't the skill to deceive his former Lord and master. Loyalty was the number one requirement with a former Lord. So Grimar wouldn't have even gotten over the drawbridge.

"The code of chivalry among them knights is the biggest jest in Europe. I mean if you were a peasant you were far more likely to get killed or raped by one them than us. The knights in their pretty tunics beat up their wives. My lord married a girl of fourteen just to get her dowry. He was an old man of forty. And when her first born was female he stood over her bed glaring and raging with anger. As if she could control the sex of the child. If she had been able to she would have given him his damn son, Peter."

"I will not insult Saint Ann like that, Mark. Just as long as the child is healthy. I can always get me a son-in law."

"My old Lord dumped his one daughter in a convent at the age of twelve. She was crying and begging him not to take her there. But he just beat her and dragged her off to the convent. A year later we heard she ran off over the border to Scotland. The lord nearly wet himself in a fit of fury. She is probably married to some Scot now. All his fellow nobles got to hear about. He was the jest of the county."

"Remember how we had to save five Scottish peasant children from them knights, who were going run though the children with their swords? Told them there was a Scottish army over the hill. They soon galloped off. All except one. Gave the peasant children knight's food and told them to run off and hide in the forest," Peter crackled with laughter as he relived the event.

The Captain overheard the story and was amazed that men who were trained killers could act in such a manner. He had thought from the start that the Emissary had chosen the wrong kind of men, now he was sure the fool had. These men wouldn't kill the Skraeling children.

The ship took a sharp dive and the Emissary lost his footing and went skidding along the west deck. The brief smile on Grimar's face was caught by Mark's observant eyes. Grimar hated the sin-seller even more than he did, so why was Grimar his companion on this voyage?

Grimar bent down to assist the Emissary to his feet.

"Emissary, you must take care of yourself for the sake of your holy mission," uttered Grimar in a pious voice loud enough for all to hear.

The ship's Captain turned at the mentioned of a holy mission. He had been told this was a voyage to judge the state of church property, which didn't sound to him like a holy mission. Though he did admit Grimar and the Emissary might perceive coin counting as a 'holy mission'. Nevertheless, he demanded at know what misguided campaign Mother church was conducting, just in case it wasn't coin counting.

"I was informed this voyage was to check on church property, Emissary. If that is not the case I demand to know what your holy mission is?" The Captain's voice was deliberately brisk, he felt he had been taken for a fool and maneuvered into accepting a long arduous voyage under false pretenses.

The Emissary sniffed at the foolish notion, the church would send him all the way to Greenland to check church property that wasn't worth having.

The Emissary sucked in his breath and pushed back his thin shoulders.

"Check property? I am here to investigate heresy," announced the Emissary in a fanatical voice, loaded with self-importance and disgusted that anyone would think that the church was so foolish to send a ship to check on worthless land and goods.

The crew heard the claim and the ship's Captain translated the Emissary words into English. The ship had just entered a fiord in

SAGA

far off Greenland, and he, his crew, and the English archers now knew they had been deceived.

"And what poof of heresy do you have Emissary?" demanded the ship's Captain in cold fury at being on a voyage with such a dire purpose.

The crew and archers intense glaring eyes rested fully on the Emissary, their anger mounting with very passing ripple in the fiord.

Vainly the Emissary explained his mission.

"In 1294 that was a riot against the church abuses in the Settlement. How can Mother Church commit abuse? In 1327 the tithe had to be collected by force. Grimar was born here and wisely left in 1327. He bears witness to the worship of the Norse Gods in this Settlement. Also a sailor on aboard a ship witnessed men from the West Settlement worshiping the Norse Gods."

The ship's Captain began to muster facts in his mind as he evaluated the situation. The English archers were here to kill heretics.

The Captain asked the grim question as he turned to Mark. "Mark, how many arrows have you?"

"Three hundred," replied Mark.

It was the answer the Captain had been dreading. He sighed and looked away before he summoned up the courage to tell the English archers what this meant.

"The population of the West Settlement is three hundred and the archers have three hundred arrows," declared the Captain in Norse and English.

Bared teeth snarled at the Emissary; the men had the appearance of wild boar ready to tear out his insides. Only Grimar stood beside him in support on the tiny ship's deck.

The ship's Captain was in trouble. Mutiny in Greenland's waters had to be avoided. Did this fool not realize that his life depended on the good graces of the crew? The sailors were of peasant stock as were the archers.

"There is not enough evidence to support a charge of heresy for everyone in the Settlement, just because a few men worship pagans Gods doesn't mean they all do," pronounced the Captain in no uncertain terms.

The Emissary was offended. A lowly ship's Captain thought that he knew more about heresy than a churchman. That in itself was heresy. The ship's Captain and his crew came from Iceland and could be of the same thinking as these Norse here in Greenland. Were they out to protect their fellow pagans? Was he in the nest of Pagans with only one true Christian soul at his side?

"Boat off the bough!" cried a sailor.

A dead body huddled over the oars of a wooden boat. The Captain ordered the grappling hook to be used to haul the boat alongside. A sailor climbed over the side and into the boat, passing up the body to waiting hands.

The ship captain studied the man. He had clearly died of exposure, probably from being washed out to sea, and then the current had flung the flimsy boat back into the fiord. A dangling ivory hammer on strip of leather about the man's neck was identified by the Emissary.

"Thor's hammer... they are heretics!" shouted the Emissary in paranoia.

The Captain and his crew couldn't argue with this firm proof of heresy.

The Captain appeared shackled with worry and apprehension when he approached Mark. He stood in front of him breathing in and out before he spoke.

"Mark, Thor's hammer—a symbol of the Norse Gods has been found around the dead man's neck—these people are heretics."

Mark explosive roars made everyone on board quake. He had been exposed to a heresy hunt. He and his men were far from being church loving souls. He was here to kill heretics down to the last man woman and child or he wouldn't have been given three hundred arrows. Unless the sin-seller was under the delusion that he and his men missed their targets.

"Children! What about the children, do you think me and my

men are going to put an arrow in a child?" demanded Mark. His fury was unabated. The puny sin-seller had organized the murder of innocent children.

Opposing a heresy hunt was to invite the church to hunt you. The Captain knew he had to graft a plan that would appease the Emissary, the archers, and his crew. Capturing children didn't pose any difficulty, what to do with them afterwards was the problem. Leaving them alone in Greenland was a slow and cruel death sentence. In Iceland and Norway no one wanted an extra mouth to feed. Like a beckon of light, the answered came to the Captain. Sell them as slaves.

"There is only one way to save the children and assist the church. Sell them as slaves in England,'" suggested the Captain in both languages.

Slavery and serfdom were bed mates to Mark and his men. They had no critical view of the children being peddled off into slavery. Peter gave an approving nod.

"Look at this land and the sea around it, those ice floes are going to multiply and then no ship will get through next year. Pond slime grass, that is what is growing on those slopes over there. Do you see any flowers sticking their heads in between the sick grass? No crops would grow here. And look at the excuse for a beach. Pebbled and dark gray soil. And where are the trees? These damn people here don't care about their children. Otherwise they would have left. These Greenlanders are terrible people, Mark. Terrible people." Peter almost wept as he spoke.

The Captain dismissed any notion to change Peter's opinion of the children parents. Driftwood was the only type of timber to make the journey to the West Settlement and it was sea-soaked wood which didn't make good building material. Greenland also had no iron ore to shape into metal for nails and axes. The ships they did possess, and sent to collect iron ore and wood, had probably got sunk by the heavier seas. A ship like his was the only chance the Settlement had of escaping the ice prison, and he only had room for forty children at most. The captain really didn't care about the children, he just wanted avoid mutiny, and the church's wrath.

"Emissary, neither my crew nor the archers will sanction the killing the children." His tone allowed no provision for disagreement.

"A bunch of maundering archers who would have made the Vikings run back to their long ships, care about heretic spawn?" The Emissary and Grimar were shocked—both had the opinion these men who were nothing more than a band of trained killers, who would happily preform rape, pillage, and murder. The priest remembered that his brother priest had ensured him that they would kill anyone for a coin. Now it seems that the rabble cared about Norse children in Greenland, who were not English.

He had to toil with heresy in far-off land, with only Grimar as a decent companion, and now he was lumbered with the delicate feelings of superbly trained killers. The Emissary's frayed nerves wavered.

Grimar was alarmed. The archers sounded like the darn Highlanders with their code of honour. Were they as good fighters as them? He doubted that. "And if we spare the heretic spawn, where would they be sold, Captain?"

He had to appease the Emissary quickly.

"They can be captured and sold into slavery in England."

The Captain praised himself for his artful lying. The ship was bound for the Orkneys unbeknown to the Emissary. The Earl of the Orkneys had a thriving smuggling ring operating between Iceland and the Orkneys, in order to dodge to King's taxes. People in Iceland and the Orkneys wished to curtail any power Norway had over them. Loyalty to the King wasn't on their agenda. The Earl of Orkneys would have the children sold off while the Emissary slept. A cash crop on two feet wouldn't slip by the Earl of the Orkneys. Serfs in England and Scotland had developed the habit of running off to towns. Serfs in the Highlands found the task of running off very daunting. Serfs living near towns further south had taken up the pastime with glee.

The Emissary was still struggling with the prospect that men who were the most feared warriors since the Vikings, were worried over the deaths of heretic children. Why would any good Christian care about the children? Grimar didn't care and he didn't? The illiterate souls on this ship had no understanding of the threat from heresy. There had been many heresy movements that shook the church. One came from the mouth of the Archbishop of Toledo, who tried to insist that Christ was the son of God by adoption. Another Spanish bishop agreed. Abelard rejected Saint Augustine's doctrine of original sin. Peter de Brays overthrew altars and burned crosses. The worst one in the Emissary's mind was Arnold of Bernice, he pushed the idea of poverty and that clerics from the Pope downward, should have only temporal power and own no property. He would leave the world empty of churches. In fact the church as he knew it wouldn't even exist. Violence was the only method to rid the world of heresy.

Submission to this rabble was unbearable, yet he faced a fully armed resistance. The idea of selling the children held some appeal. He could agree to their foolish demands and once the ship was safely into port at Iceland, he would have the heretic children disposed of. This was just a temporary defeat and he could live with that.

"Very well. I suppose we should give the children a chance to convert. There is no greater glory than converting a pagan," agreed the Emissary.

The Captain told Mark of the Emissary's agreement.

Mark automatically knew the Emissary was offering an olive branch that the sin-seller meant to take back later. Mark was amused at the Emissary's stupid blunder. Mark guessed the reason for the man's confidence was that he thought the ship was going to dock in Iceland, where he commanded the power of rank. Peter was still stewing in anger and he finally erupted.

"St. Ann said in church...my future wife is here in Greenland I can't have her killed!"

The Captain and the archers stared at Peter, thinking he had lost his mind. The Captain turned to the Emissary.

"The archer Peter says St. Ann told him he would find his future wife in Greenland, while he was in church," the Captain was very shaken by Peter's statement.

Much to everyone's surprise, the Emissary took the matter seriously and called Peter over to talk with him.

"Ask him to explain."

The captain translated the Emissary's order.

"I was in a church in England and I prayed to my St. Ann and it came to me that I would find my future-wife in a green-land. St. Ann has never let me down. So she is here. I won't have her killed," protested Peter.

The Captain told Emissary what Peter had told him word for word. The Emissary was impressed by Peter's faith and to disregard the verdict of a Saint was unthinkable. St. Ann would surely send them a sigh that the female was a true Christian.

"St. Ann sent a message in the house of God, it must be obeyed, tell him so, and St. Ann will give us a sign of who she is. His future wife will be saved," said in the Emissary in a sanctimonious tone.

The Captain translated the Emissary words to Peter who breathed freely at the news.

Mark's mouth twisted in disgust. This normally logical friend believed a cryptic message in church, straight after coming from battle with the Scots. The sin-seller who wouldn't spare a child, would spare a woman on the basis of jumbled message from St. Ann. Peter could get a wife in England. Mark was really bothered that his old comrade in arms was going lumber himself with some dumpy inbreed female from this Settlement, just because he had a moment of madness. One glance at his friend's face told Mark it was not a wise idea to instill sense into Peter about his future wife. He was in love with a female who didn't exist. He wasn't going help Peter find her. A nice girl in England with a dowry was what Peter needed.

"She wouldn't have a dowry, Peter."

"Do I need one? I got money selling that dead knight's horse, his sword and what he had in his purse. I will buy some land for sheep in Northumberland. Going to have one of them, two level homes, one day. My children will all be able to read and write, Mark."

Peter's outlandish plans made Mark wonder if he had suffered a head injury in battle. The other archers sneered at Peter.

"Why work on a farm? We have all been serfs. There is easy money to be had in France and Scotland for men like us. Just shoot an arrow," said one young archer.

Mark considered him even more lost to reason than Peter. Sure there was wealth to be had from loot, but was there was also the risk of death or life long injury. Luck always ran out. He was going to retire, but not to a farm.

Grimar was troubled. He had been looking forward to torturing the children, listening to their howls for mercy and demented screams, now they were going to live. Sold as slaves their life wouldn't be any harder than here in Greenland.

"Emissary the children will be infected with heresy unless they are very young," he whispered in panic.

"We will be docking in Iceland and there they will be properly disposed of. Just let these idiots think they have won. We need them to get rid of the heretics. Once in Iceland we won't be requiring their services. Trust me Grimar, I can out think the English archers."

Grimar had no faith in the Emissary being able to out think anyone. Much less a trained a killer with eyes that wandered over details, which was what Mark was.

Besides the Captain had informed him about the people of Iceland, and they would never condone the murder of children. Most of them adhered to insipid Norse customs. The Emissary was more likely to be killed by them. The children were going to live, along with the female Peter wanted for a wife. Grimar faced the sad fact that he was going to have to sneak around and the children alone. The archers would be busy, and the Emissary was too stupid to know what he was doing. The man reminded him of his in-laws. They were so shocked when they found themselves tied up ready to be skinned. Both in-laws died from shock, and he got no pleasure from this, like he did from throwing his wife off of the cliff. Grimar noted the change in Mark's manner. The killer archer was getting prepared for battle.

Mark turned his mind to tactics for the deceitful campaign against the peasants, who were under the delusion that their king had sent a ship for peaceful purposes. Was the Emissary capable of tactical battle? Mark shrugged. His body rippled with muscles and was as stout as an oak tree. His blue eyes sparkling, he flicked back his short brown hair and scratched at his short beard. He walked steadily over to the Captain.

"Captain does the Emissary actually have any strategy for his fumbling plans?" inquired Mark sucking in air between his teeth.

The Captain had also assumed the Emissary lacked a basic knowledge of strategy. The dour church man had accepted a sinister mission and therefore the duty to oversee the mission belonged to him alone. Totally impertinent, the Captain went up to the Emissary and tapped him on the shoulder.

"Strategy. The mission is yours and the archers need to know your tactics. You're the commander not them Emissary."

The Emissary mistook the statement for flattery. His neck took a slow upward diagonal path with an air of conceit. Men waited on his superior judgment.

"Of course, I have a map of the settlement and will give orders on where to strike," the Emissary removed a map from his leather bag.

"The Godthaab fiord and the adjoining Kangersuneq Fiord will be our first port of call. They will be invited to attend the church as the King wished to re-settle the community. In Vinland where two large uninhabitable islands have been found, so the heretics will be told. Of course none have been found as no one has looked. Should they not wish to live in Vinland, they will be told there is the option of returning to Iceland. Of course there is no such option. I will give mass, and the wine will have hemlock in it. Grimar as bravely volunteered to go the Sandnes farm and give them the same tale. Except Grimar will tell them there will be a meeting will be at

Pointed Rocks. A very good place for an ambush according to Grimar. I don't have enough hemlock. I purchased three hundred arrows to allow for the archers missing a few targets. Not because I intended to use all the arrows to eliminate all the heretics," informed the Emissary as if he were conversing with stupid people.

The tone of voice and his manner didn't impress Mark even though the Captain hadn't yet translated the Emissary's words. The Captain was nervous as he translated the Emissary plan to Mark.

Mark sneered, the Emissary was loathsome. The thought poison being given to the victims was most unmanly. Not the way of a warrior. His Lord had never resorted to it. Scotland's men didn't either. The Emissary was a coward to use such a method. But did shorten the time he and his men would spend in this ice cage and he wanted to leave with all possible haste.

His men grouped around in the rear of the ship to discuss the plan.

"It is the sort of plan I'd expect him to come up with. He can't fight and he wouldn't. He is a coward. The only living thing he could kill would be children, who couldn't fight back. I have seen men like him before in France and Scotland," remarked Peter.

"France won't be seeing me. I am buying a boat sailing up and down the river," informed Mark with pride.

His friends stared at him with gapping mouths. Mark, their chief archer, was going to become river-boat sailor.

The serious expression on Mark's face repressed any desire to exhibit a humorous remark or laugh at his announcement. Peter breathed slowly and then set about serving up a dish of hard reality.

"Can you sail a boat Mark?"

"One of the crew wants to join me," Mark was engrossed in his future life. Visions of sailing his boat down the steady river water, watching the landscape change as his boat wound its way round the snake like river, it was very pleasant. The most pleasant aspect of new employment was being able to dodge nosy sin-sellers sniffing for coins and confessions. Mark looked over at the Emissary, the thought of evading any more of his replicas, was more delicious than ale.

"A sailor wants to join you?" asked Peter.

"Can you blame him after this voyage? And he wants a warmer climate. The Captain is quitting too. He is off to the Orkneys to just do short trips between the islands and Scotland. Greenland has disturbed many men on this ship."

"Not Grimar and the Emissary—they were both disturbed at birth," sniggered Peter.

Grimar thought of Ingrid as he looked out over the water, she would make a dangerous foe, if she were still alive. Thorfinn had to take first place on his list of foes though. Thorfinn had been the same age as himself in 1327. His family really were followers of the Norse Gods. He felt the man was still alive on his farm in the Itivdlek Fiord. Getting to Thorfinn and his family to the meeting would be difficult. An ambush was the only way to snuff the air out of Thorfinn's lungs. Grimar wanted Thorfinn alive however, so he could watch his family die slowly.

Mark watched Grimar, and for a moment Grimar's mental barriers were down. The moment was enough for Mark to penetrate them and see the real Grimar. The man had come here to kill and torture for revenge. He was mad. The children and Peter's wife would be in grave danger from Grimar.

"Peter, see that Grimar looks insane, I saw it in his eyes. He is not just traitor, but mad. He will try to kill the children and wife of yours. He's mad, just as you said."

Peter was aghast. Peasant children and his wife in danger from the mad man! To kill him might bring them under suspicion. But what if they put Grimar in a situation where someone else could be kill or injure him? The thought of Grimar as a cripple was quite pleasing. Death was the better option for Grimar. Come what may, Grimar had to be kept away from the children and his future wife. Saint Ann would never bless him again if he didn't keep Grimar under close watch. Mark was much better at dealing with people that he was. He could hear a man tread ground and walk as silent as a wolf, but people puzzled him. Peasants everywhere had it so hard, while the nobles and the likes of Grimar had it so good. When and what would put it right?

The ship steered to into the heart of Kangersuneq Fiord.

Two men who were fishing nearly dropped their oars in shock at the sight of the vessel with the King's standard flying from the mast. It had been sixteen years since a ship had sailed into these waters. The two men were only three years old when that happened, but they still remembered it and the damage it caused. Over the years the winters had grown harsher, and it was no longer possible for anyone to stay in the West Settlement. No matter how great the risk, they had to leave. Before their eyes was transport. Far better transport than Thorfinn's ship. Two hundred people could fit on that ship. It was made of stout oak and proper nails from decent iron ore created, by skilled craftsmen in a good forge.

The Captain was very pleased to see a pair of sailors in a runt of boat. They could spread the news and debate on why the ship had come. He doubted whether such primitive souls would come to figure out why. Their brains were as frozen as Greenland, which is why they had turned their back on the Norse Gods.

Mark too had seen the boat. He opted to concentrate on his mission, which would enable him and his men to leave Greenland, and its peculiar folk. The captain steered towards the boat and spread the news.

"It's the ship we were told about?" yelled a youth almost in tears.

"Let us go and greet it!" shouted the other youth, his wild joyful voice bounced off the cliffs.

The youths raced to reach the miracle afloat in the West Settlement. Their hearts skipped a beat when the ship turned directly into the boat's path. The youths shouted up to the ship.

"Are you off course?"

The captain smiled and bellowed back.

"No, we are a Royal ship on a mission of good will, unlike the ship in 1327. Captain Harkonson had been in the smuggling trade for years and knew what the men wanted to hear.

The Emissary stepped up to the rail and called down to the

youths with a look of piety and Christian charity.

"Go and tell the people to gather at the church!"

"They are already there, to talk about leaving the Settlement. They held a gathering at the church. Then a boat arrived saying they had spotted you. I doubt if the outlaying farms know about your ship-there are four of them."

The Emissary shuddered. The heretics would use a house of God for such lowly unimportant affairs, instead of offering prayer and thanks to God? His inflexible thoughts made him forget to ask why such a meeting was being held and why they wanted to leave.

Grimar was alert to the fact a catastrophe had occurred, otherwise a meeting would not have been held. He interrupted the Emissary to obtain decent information.

"Why is a meeting be held in the Settlement?

The youths looked up from the boat with sadness in their eyes and answered.

"Every child under eight died last winter and every pregnant woman. There are only 210 people left alive and fewer than seventy are under thirteen years of age."

The hardened sailors were momentarily touched by the calamity that had befallen the West Settlement. The Captain was somewhat relieved that all the younger children had died. He couldn't have taken any children under three and didn't want to kill babies.

"It would take us too long to stop at every outlying farm. We have to get the word back to the church meeting that you are coming and it isn't like it was in 1327. Can you stop at the farms?" asked the older youth.

"Yes we can, and will I think," replied the Emissary.

Grimar flanked the Emissary's side, sighing at the belief that he had to think of everything. Was the pious prattler not capable of thinking about details.

"How many children are alive in each Fiord?" inquired Grimar.

"Godthaab and Kangersuneq Fiords there eighteen children under thirteen, twenty three in Pisigsarfix. In the Lysu Fiord area there are twenty one children. Eight in the Itivdlek Fiord.

"Thorfinn is taking a ship to Vinland. Silly folk, they might change their minds when they hear you are on the way."

"A woman called Ingrid use to live near her is she still alive?' asked Grimar.

"No, she died years ago."

Grimar held back the relief that rushed through him. Grimar's most powerful foe was dead. Ingrid the witch was the only one who could have stopped him. No one else had her skill. Thorfinn and his people were too wrapped in the Norse Gods to command enough respect. Entrenched Christian doctrine was going to be the death of them. Grimar had put his hand over his mouth. It required effort to choke back his laughter.

The Emissary had taken note of the mention of the ship and the voyage to Vinland.

"Where does this Thorfinn live Grimar?" muttered the Emissary.

"Thorfinn lives in the Itivdlek Fiord Emissary. His father was violent and so were the men in that fiord. Vile murderers as I remember. I shudder every time I recall the events. Leaving here was a blessing. It was priest who saved me from this place. To work in the fields of the Orkneys with God fearing people was a blessing," lied Grimar with a glowing smile of remembrance on his face.

Mark couldn't understand what was said, but he did notice the expression of Grimar's unmasked hate, fleeting as it was.

The Captain was relieved that Mark and men couldn't understand the Norse language. Had they been able to they would have classed the people as peasants like themselves and he would once again would face a mutiny.

The Captain began to worry his supplies didn't stretch to feeding that many children. He shook himself for not thinking about that earlier. Still living on a bit of fish may keep them alive. It was all they would be getting, but his crew came first.

"Go and spread the word we are not the same as the ship in 1327" ordered the Emissary in all honesty.

"That we will gladly," the youths were overjoyed at being saved, and they pulled hard and fast on the oars, rowing away.

Grimar noticed smoke coming from a farm. He remembered it has being the most isolated farm in Kangersuneq Fiord.

"Emissary, look at the smoke over there. It is first farm in Kangersuneq Fiord. Chances are they haven't received an invite to this gathering."

The Emissary had no intentions of allowing one heretic to escape if he could help it. God and his Saints would not forgive such failures in duty.

"Captain, pull into the shoreline below that farm house," ordered the Emissary.

The Captain complied with the order. A young boy dressed in skins and barefoot was gathering driftwood on the shoreline. His mouth dropped open and he stared wide eyed in wonder at a sight his young eyes had never seen before.

"Oh!" was the only sound he made. He had heard sagas mention ships, but he never seen one.

The Captain came ashore in small boat with the Emissary, Peter, and Mark.

"Where are your parents boy?" demanded the Emissary.

The boy didn't answer. He was engrossed in the fine black tunic and silver trimming worn by the Emissary. It was such splendid clothing he couldn't take his eyes off of it.

"The boy is in awe at the sight of the Emissary's attire, he will regain his attention in few moments" explained Mark.

The Captain related Mark's theory to the Emissary who had no patience with heretic's spawn.

"They are dead. Only me and my sister up on the hill here," said the boy. He forgot to mention that his parents had only just died in the last three days, and no one in the Settlement knew of their deaths.

The Captain's shocked face alerted Mark to the fact that the boy had given unpleasant news and the Captain quickly relayed what the boy had said to him.

"I told you these people were low and evil," snapped Peter.

"Call your sister down here boy," commanded the Captain.

"Gunnhild, come on down!" shouted twelve year old Einar.

A girl of ten years came running down the hill. She too wore skins. Her hair was matted and she was bare foot. Peter and Mark admired her for being able to run bare foot over such cold land. A real peasant child. Good thing they had arrived to save her.

The Emissary stopped and looked at the first heretic spawn he seen. He felt a shiver go through him. She would drown off the coast of Iceland. Mark picked up the on hate the Emissary had for the peasant child and nudged Peter.

Mark and Peter shook their heads thinking it was a great pity that couldn't put an arrow in the sin-seller. As they were a short distance away from him, they spoke freely.

"You know his friend, that priest back in England is living near you, Peter. If we can't kill the sin-seller, we could get his fellow sin-seller in England."

"I'll be giving him to Scots then, they can be very obliging them, Scots when it comes to getting rid of the unwanted," Peter smirked. His wide lips made him looked quite hideous.

"For someone who follows St. Ann, you are not too religious, Peter."

"My Saint Ann won't want the Emissary and his friend. She is fussy," assured Peter, gravely intolerant of any insult to his Saint.

Peter's version of the Christian faith didn't trouble Mark. He knew many people who thought exactly like Peter. He liked the Church just not the people who ran it. One day hopeful something would be done with the rabble that operated the Church.

"Come boy, and bring your sister. We will take you on my ship," ordered the Captain.

Einar and Gunnhild strolled over to the boat and sat quietly until it reached the ship. Einar and Gunnhild impressed the sailors with their climbing ability. Gunnhild smiled at everyone the second her feet touched the deck. Mark and Peter climbed up and leaped over the rail. The Captain saw no point in tying the children up as they seemed too happy to be on the ship.

"Saint Ann will be pleased we saved them," remarked Peter

delighted, with the children's response.

Gunnhild and Einar were so happy they began to sing a hymn. It was the only song they knew. The Emissary was stunned the children were Christians. That explained why no one had taken the orphans in their homes. He asked God's forgiveness for his hasty judgment.

"To think Grimar, Christian children living alone. Abandoned by the people living here," expressed the Emissary in total dismay.

Fully aware of the close ties people had with one another in this Norse community, Grimar doubted that the children had been abandoned. He wasn't too bothered at being unable to torture this pair, as there would plenty of other juicy pickings to be had. The first one was within sight. Grimar saw the farm house on the hill.

High on the hill top stood two women. They saw the wonderful white sail bellowing in the wind. They released a wailing cry as they were on the verge of being rescued. The women continued to shed tears of joy for a few minutes.

"A ship. A ship after all these years. One has finally come we don't have to spend another winter here. Or rely on Thorfinn to come and take us to Vinland," gasped one woman, holding her hand to her mouth.

"I had no faith in a follower of Thor coming back for us. His ship in no way measures up to the long ships of old," commented a man who had come to join them. The Royal ship was a liberator to his eyes.

"Well we don't have to rely on him a Royal ship has come," sobbed a woman.

"Vinland—with Thorfinn and his mob? No thanks. My son is all I have left and I want him to live in civilized land. Iceland is for me. None of those stinking Skraeling will trouble us there. And Thorfinn is very friendly with them savages," snarled a man. He despised Thorfinn and the Norse Gods. He was a devoted Christian and his heart was in the homelands.

"We had bad dealings with King and Church in 1327," infused a man gripped with doubt about the intentions of the men on the

King's ship.

"That was then! That King is probably dead. He must else why would a ship come. They can't be here to rob us. They must realize we don't have anything. Unless they want some driftwood," the woman held up a small sea soaked log. Laughter broke out and rational thoughts departed from their minds.

"Oh—here it comes", she shouted and danced as the ship anchored.

"What a fool Thorfinn is. Building his stupid ship. That is a real ship. We are saved. Thanks be to God!" yelled the man with so much joy tears had formed in his eyes.

The Emissary donned on black cloak and gazed at the heretics waving to him. Their deceit wouldn't save them. He had been trained in the devil's ways.

Mark hoped his victims would descend down the hill to meet them. He counted two women, six men, and two children, all of whom were too close to each other to send a hail of arrows into the air without killing the children.

"Separate the children from the adults," ordered Mark to the Captain.

The Emissary was perplexed on how to separate the children from the adults. Mark noticed the dithering sin-seller. He looked to the Captain, who nodded and decided to take over the operation. The two young children who seemed to be about ten and eight years old could fetch a nice few coins on the auction block.

"Let the children come aboard and have a look at the ship," called out the Captain from the boat as it drew within yards from the shoreline.

The women smiled and nodded with affection to the children. They raced over the terrain laughing and yelling with delight at every stride they took. Their faces were beaming with complete joy as they were taken to the ship. The ten year old boy stared in wonder at the mast. It must be much taller and thicker than Thorfinn's ship, and it was also wider and longer. Not that he had seen Thorfinn's ship, but his imagination told him the Royal ship had to be better. What an adventure it would be to sail on such a ship, becoming a sailor was his greatest wish. To see new lands and strange sights. The boy envied the sailors their lifestyle. The girl just looked around. Her only wish was to live in a warmer land with no long dark winters.

Mark, Peter, and one other archer wandered down the shoreline. None of the Greenlanders took the slightest note—they were all gathered round the Emissary. The dithering Emissary made an excuse to return to the boat.

The women and men chatted while their eyes focused on the Emissary. The archers released their deadly cargo, they all fell to the ground dead. The children screamed at the sight but were held back by the strong arms of the sailors on the ship's deck.

Peter and Mark could see the children. It didn't disturb Mark and his men. They had done their duty to the peasant children, whether they escaped or not was in their own hands now. Life in England was just that life. The boy would most likely spend his days in the fields belonging to some lazy lord. The girl too would share her brother's fate.

"They don't know how lucky they are," said Peter.

"Well we gave those dim wits as quick a death as we could," said Mark as he watched the dead bodies on the water. He was proud that he always tried for a clean quick kill. Of course on a battle field with wall of arrows flying through the air, it simply wasn't possible. It didn't upset him however, he never gave it a thought.

Peter and the other archer returned to the boat. Mark was alone as he walked up to the stone farm house. He growled in scorn at the land. It was unable to support crops and animals—he hadn't seen any chickens or pigs—how could anyone live here? The whole place hadn't got a single tree and these cruel people kept their children in such a land. All of the youngest ones had died and still the worthless parents hadn't left. He had no pity for the dead being rolled into the sea by Grimar. But his confidence was too high and he neglected to stay alert.

A man armed with a swinging an axe appeared before him.

Mark had used up his arrows, his only defense was a long thin dagger at his side.

"You again, and have come to kill again like you did in 1327! And you have got my boy and my brother's girl on your damn evil ship! Thorfinn will have your innards, demon!" he cursed and raved.

Mark dismissed the words. He couldn't understand them and walked slowly backwards towards the house. The man's feet didn't move with any dexterity. This foe blustering in front of him had never fought in battle. With nimble feet Mark danced leisurely from side to side, almost laughing at his opponent's attempt to slice him with an axe.

"You damn coward, you won't fight!" he swung his axe.

Mark's opponent worked himself into a frenzy, lunging with his axe. The sound of the axe swishing through the air didn't unnerve Mark. His face was expressionless as his back touched the stone wall of the house.

"Got you coward, nowhere to run now!" with all his strength the man swung his axe.

Mark darted to the left at the very last second and the axe hit the stone wall. Mark had danced round and was at the man's back with his dagger slicing the attacker's throat. Blood gushed like fountain as the Greenlander fell back, gurgling in his death throes.

"Should have fought like that to get your family out of this hell hole," shouted Mark in rage as he stood over the dying man.

The boy on the ship had seen what had happened and how his father had fought for him and his young cousin. Tears of remorse fell like rain, until hate dug in its claws. This horde of killers hadn't encountered the settlement's best fighters yet. Thorfinn and his men—they would take this ship it was going end up in Thorfinn's hands. The thought brought an evil grin to the boy.

"You will be got," snapped the boy with hands tied.

The Captain gazed at the boy and decided that some discipline had to be administered. He picked up a rope and lashed the boy across his arms with it.

"You speak when spoken to slave!"

Grimar was gloating over the dead and sucked the blood off of the arrows pulled out of their chests, before he rolled the bodies down to the sea and watched them splash into the water. Mark pondered on what other obscene acts he was going to have to witness.

Einar and Gunnhild trembled in terror in the rear of the ship. These men were here to kill. Why? What had the people in the Settlement done? Niether of the children had seen anyone other than their parents for a year. Einar felt because he was a male and head of the family, that it was his duty to protect his sister. He experienced a warning inside his head that he had to keep quiet and obey the Captain. Or he and Gunnhild would be joining the boy and girl bound up at the rear of the ship.

The ship sailed on to its next target.

Two glum individuals were combing the shoreline for driftwood and any bits of bone that they could find. A tiny ice floe brought forth sniffling sobs. The deaths of two women and five children had left just a skeleton of hope.

"Not another winter like the last one. Please God, my wife is dead; me and my brother have two boys left to us. Oh God please, please," the man fell on his knees on tiny smooth stones that littered the shoreline pleading to God for mercy.

The two boys were greatly trouble by their fathers' dark foreboding pain. They gulped and stayed with the logs, they had found a few yards away. The ship came into sight— joy chimed in the boys' throats.

"Fathers look….it's a ship. We are saved! We are saved."

Optimism caused them to forge wild dreams, and to forget the past.

"It is a ship we will soon be gone. Soon be we'll be free of Greenland!" said the fathers as they stood in reverence at the spectacle of the royal ship.

The boys ran to join their fathers and they commenced a joyous dance on wet pebbles beneath their feet. Their martyrdom in the white hell was at an end. The white sail was being lower and was coming to deliver to them to the promised land of Iceland.

"Will soon be in Iceland!" remarked one man, devoid of all reality. Their savior was coming.

***

Mark was aware of the black art of Grimar's tongue and he didn't care to witness any unnecessary more lies from it. Mark and Peter applied two arrows to their bows and sent wooden shafts on flight over the deep water. The freak action destroyed all hope in the boys. Their fathers lay dead alongside them, with open eyes and mouths. The boys railed almost instantly and took flight. Peter and Mark admired the boys' ability to cover a good distance before being over taken, and the amount of force needed to subdue them.

"Those pair will escape one day from any would-be master," grinned Peter with earnest approval.

The ship traveled down the fiord. Three Norsemen were engaged in a battle with some native folk. Arrows pieced Greenland's rotten soil, without claiming a single victim. Both parties had taken cover behind rocks, and were of equal number and skill.

"A local raid, reminds me of Scots," commented Peter, rather enjoying watching somebody else's fight from the safe distance of the ship's deck. Mark scratched his head and shouted.

"Grimar!"

Always happy to lounge in the centre of attention, he quickly answered the summons. He was only too aware that he alone could give light on the event happening on the shoreline.

"The ones on the left are Skraeling. They often raid Norse animals and fights break out. Only the people on Itivdlek Fiord ever managed to get on with the Skraeling," said Grimar. The Captain interrupted his words.

"And the Itivdlek Fiord folk are the ones who want to go to Vinland? Well they are likely to be successful. If they get there. Which they won't, unless they have the good sense to run," speculated Mark with glint of amused malice; he was unreserved in his disrespect for the fighting proficiency of any Greenlander.

The Captain began to envy Mark's lavish insight into human behaviour. He and the Earl of the Orkneys had outperformed the slippery tricks of the King's tax collector. But he was willing to confess he was an amateur compared to Mark.

The men behind the rocks let a out round of cheers.

"Look a ship! You Skraeling will run now," growled a man he waved to the ship.

The shrilling cries made by the worthless wretches didn't procure one fragment of mercy in Mark's heart. Wisely the Inuit began to cautiously withdraw from the conflict.

Mark and his men sent arrows whirling on Greenland's wind from the ship's deck.

The men thought the arrows were being aimed at the Skraeling and laughed until three arrows head plunged through the cavities of their chests, tearing apart tissue and organs. But even while they were dying they thought it was an accident.

Mark, one of his men and two sailors entered the stone turf house on the hill. Putrid rotting flesh and the smell of excrement filled the men's nostrils, the moment the door was half ajar.

A woman laid dead, and a boy about nine with hollow cheeks and eyes set deep in his head stared up at Mark from the dirt floor. The boy's moving lips proved to Mark he was still alive, but near death. Mark quickly bent down and scooped up the boy.

"Those men fought raiders while these two lay dying of hunger," spat Mark with venom and sour disgust, as he carried the thin boned boy down the slope.

"You useless trio," he spat as he passed the dead bodies.

Two Inuit men heading for the house, halted at the sight of men dressed very differently to the Norsemen. The strangers had killed their enemies. One Inuit man took the chance and waved to the archers.

Peter waved back merrily. The Inuit men walked off over the hill.

On the deck Einar's sought to unravel the conflicting images of this warrior with a six foot high bow. The warrior could kill without hesitation or anger, and yet he carried a boy in his arms. The boy looked near death from hunger. "Why the children, and not the adults?" asked Einar in silence. Einar recalled a Viking who flatly refused to kill children. Was this strange warrior from a distance land like that Viking of old?

"Keep quiet Gunnhild and be calm," advised prudent Einar.

On the ship Mark placed the boy on a full soft sack to support his weak body. Peter put a spoon full of minced fish into the child's mouth. A sailor placed half a cup of ale down the boy. The child's breathing started to become firmer.

"More proof these people are heretics," snapped the Emissary staring down at the boy on the sack. Mark up a fur over the boy.

"Do you die believing in Christ's Grace, boy?" asked the Emissary in a stern voice.

The Captain opted not to translate the words to the English archer, who was already longing for violence. The Emissary's words would not be well received by the men, who held no love for this priest.

Einar, who could understand the priest, began to think the pagans he had heard about in Itivdlek Fiord, might be more sensible. Einar's family had made infrequent visits to hear Halfdan speak about the Saints, which only bored Einar, and now he was confronted with this macabre spectacle. Thorfinn's people worshiped the Norse Gods, Einar elected to give Thor a try. "Mighty Thor, I am young and need wisdom to know how to behave with these peculiar people and what path to take. Mighty Thor, I hope you will consider my request", prayed Einar in silence.

Einar saw the ship approach another farm. He yearned to cry a warning, but that would sentence his sister to death. Only Thorfinn and his men could tackle the warriors on this ship.

A small family was fishing on the shoreline in a tiny cove. Resilience was fading in their hearts. Life's hardship had produce an atmosphere where any thread of hope would be clutched at and trust willing given.

"A ship—it's coming into our tiny cove! Oh Lord God I give you thanks. This is a wonderful day. They are launching a boat. Come everyone let us hurry to meet them," the woman pushed back her hair trying to look her best. Hysterical joy ran through her.

The small family hurried long the shoreline of the tiny cove's beach, their wishes fulfilled by their faith in a loving God. Christ in his mercy had sent a ship to transport them out of Greenland.

Grimar and five archers were in the boat.

"I am Grimar. I used to live here. We haven't come for taxes or tithe. No need to fear, the old King is dead."

"Oh I knew it wasn't going to be a repeat of 1327," said the man to his wife as he stood on the wind swept shoreline watching the boat draw ever nearer.

"This is a small farm, there is only us here to welcome you," added his wife wishing to impress the visitors.

Grimar's expression changed to express his disappointment.

The girl was jumping up and down.

"Can I come on your ship?"

Grimar stepped ashore and smiled.

"Oh yes—if your parents say so while I speak with them."

"Go on daughter," said his father happy, to give consent.

Merrily the girl's bare feet ran through the ankle high water and climbed into the boat with the archers.

"Are you in the King's service?" asked the girl. Her joy faded when they didn't answer. She didn't take too much notice and watched the men with bows.

"Your friends are silly. Nothing will attack them here." assured the girl.

The girl sprang to her feet and almost toppled out of the boat when two arrows flew into her parent's chests.

"What..."

Powerful arms tried to pull her back down into the boat, but the girl was in the water and swam for the shoreline. The sailors rowed back to the shore. Mark jumped out of the boat and sped after her.

"Help Gorm! Royal ship is attacking us!" she yelled as she ran.

Her shouting warned Mark that not all his targets were dead. Over the rise came a young man with a spear in hand.

"Back are you, you vile maggots!" the man raged while he ran down the slope, yelling with his spear aimed at Mark.

"Get behind me, girl," he ordered.

The young girl raced behind the man with the spear.

He lunged forward trying to stab Mark. He grabbed the spear, and swung it around with ease. Gorm was impaled on his own spear.

"Can't any of you fight?" mocked Mark as he screwed the spear round in the man's gut. Blood poured from his mouth and chest. Terror gripped the girl so much she was unable to move. Mark reached her and slung her over his shoulder.

"You are going to live," he said gently patting the girl's head.

Grimar went ashore. He stood over the corpses.

"Must have been a shock eh," teased Grimar as he bent down and ripped the arrows from their chest. Then Grimar kicked the dead bodies along the shoreline and into the sea.

The girl gazed with eyes filled with horror as the cold waters of the fiord claimed the bodies of her parents. The boat pulled up to the ship. Mark carried her on board and placed her on the deck.

Why?" wailed the girl looking at bodies of her parents in the water.

"Heretic spawn, you will obey or feel the lash!" threatened the Emissary looking down at the girl, he did wish to drown her. He felt sad that the girl was alive here on the deck, not in the cold water with her heretic parents.

"You are all to be sold a slaves," injected the Captain.

Slaves—this was a slave ship and it didn't want her parents. Soon it would leak out and the Settlement would rally to free the.

Peter ignored the girl as just another causality of war, and he had that many times in his twenty two years of life. He and Mark had been fighting since the age of fourteen.

Peter's intense vision saw the puny semi-circle stone rubble beach with cold green water that trickled over its shoreline. Forest people moved out of areas that were a danger to their children, these loafers couldn't be bothered. The backward and lazy Greenlanders had to be among the worst parents he had ever encountered. Peter reflected that many believed the church doctrine of beating a child was good and necessary. Those people would get on well with these low-life Greenlanders. Somewhere in the cold slime of this 'green-land', was his future wife. Someone to be his companion and share his hopes and dreams, was suffering in this hole at the end of the earth. She would love a house with a chimney, and a feather bed too.

Peter's vision became fixed on yet another Greenland farm.

On the shoreline twenty six year old Cnut had been agonizing whether to go with Thorfinn, or chance an overland journey to the East Settlement. His daughter Freydis was all he had left. The Skraeling might kill her in Vinland. No one had very been able to live in Vinland. The place was alive with thousands of Skraeling. Yet winter had crushed the life from the young and it would do it again. A overland journey of two hundred and fifty mile could also kill the girl of nine. Deliberation had to end. Action was required before the summer sun started to dim and obliterate the chance to do anything.

Then the Royal ship sailing around the bend. Cnut's breath stopped. He was so glad he hadn't opted to go with Thorfinn. A finely built ship had come to rest on the fiord by his farm. Cnut's friends waved and shouted with joy at the ship.

Grimar almost laughed when he leaned against the ship's rail and looked out over the water to observe the next lot of fools at the water's edge, waving to the ship. He would be kicking their dead bodies into the water in a few minutes.

Grimar inhaled deeply as he recognized the red haired man waving from the shoreline. A red haired boy had bullied him as a child. It was Cnut. He wouldn't be calling him Grimar the Fool anymore. The girl at his side was also red haired, and must be his daughter. Grimar yearned to flay her and listen to her screams, pleading to be set free, then finally begging for death. Unfortunately he would have to wait. It was useless unless he could get her alone. It was possible. Who would object if he grabbed the girl? The thought nourished his mounting sadistic perversity.

"Emissary, let me go with you to meet the heretics."

"Must I go ashore with you?" The Emissary wallowed in self-pity. The proposition of mixing with the heretics even for short time, could expose him to danger. Certainly he would have to endure the experience when they docked off the other fiords, but this was unnecessary. Grimar ushered the Emissary off the ship and into the boat.

"Cnut, old friend it's me—Grimar!" called out Grimar in a friendly greeting from the boat. Grimar was dressed in good attire, and to think he had called him Grimar the Fool. The jest was on him for being a fool. Cnut was happy to see Grimar. His old friend had braved angry seas to bring aid. Grimar's loyalty and courage so nothing short of marvelous. Men would write a saga about him. After being absent for sixteen years Grimar hadn't forgotten his people in West Greenland. Grimar had brought ship to save them. Grimar must be a man of great importance to be able to influence a King. Or he had carried out a great deed on the behalf of Norway, just as he was doing now for his friends. Cnut felt proud to call him a friend. His daughter Freydis would live due to Grimar's sacrifice. It was a debt he could never repay.

"Grimar, you look to be a wealthy man," said Cnut in admiration.

"One of our own has come back to help us," shouted the woman at his side.

"A son of the Settlement has come to put things right," declared a man on the left in with gratitude at Grimar's noble deed.

The words sang sweetly in Grimar's ear. Mark was in the boat when he realized that the people regarded the maggot dung as a friend when really he was a traitor. The lowest form of life was a traitor. It was the first time Mark felt pity for the Greenlanders. But his only duty was to his men and his dream of new life in England, not some Greenlander who refused to relocate.

Grimar wanted to relish every moment of his encounter with his old tormentor, Cnut. The man rushed forward and hugged Grimar.

"Haven't you done well. Look at all that fine green attire," congratulated Cnut without malice as if he were talking to long lost friend.

The three adults and Freydis gathered around Grimar welcoming him home and asking a myriad of questions. They laughed and thanked Grimar for thinking of them.

"Are you married Grimar?" asked Cnut.

"My wife died just a few months ago. I have a daughter Jean with the same red hair your daughter has. Took after her mother thankfully—mine is just dull brown,' jested Grimar, loving the deceit.

"We lost very pregnant woman last winter."

"Yes, we heard that from two men out fishing," said Grimar in a sympathetic tone.

"You know then that we must leave, if you could just take the children?"

"Oh...we will take the children."

"Grimar that is wonderful!" exclaimed Cnut in humble gratitude.

The archers had turned their backs on the crowd. Grimar was tied of his charade and walked towards the boat. Cnut was puzzled but thought Grimar must be going to collect something from the boat. Grimar climbed into the boat he laughed mockingly.

"But you will be staying!"

Cheerful looks were replaced by bewilderment at the remark—until the archers turned and fired. Cnut was the only one standing with two arrows in his chest and blood oozing from body. The Emissary had foolishly stayed ashore. Dying, Cnut with knife in hand, staggered towards the Emissary.

Mark saw the depth of the water which would cover the witless priest if he fell in, and their beloved hard won money would find a permanent home in Greenlander's horrid waters instead of bringing comfort to him and his men. Mark hurdled over the dead bodies and pounced onto Cnut's chest, pushing the arrow into the lung cavity and forcing him to the ground. Still Cnut fought on and the men lay locked in bodily combat, rolling over and over, until death finally claimed Cnut.

"Well you were a warrior—just like your Viking ancestors," commented Mark as he clamored to his feet and stood over the dead body.

"Dear Lord..." wailed the Emissary as he swayed in shock and was barely able to stand upright.

Freydis raced along the shoreline. Grimar was intoxicated with sadism and pursued the girl. His elation mounted when the girl sped round a bend out of the sight of the men.

"Your father use to call me Grimar the Fool. But you won't."

"Father...Grimar...you are a...demon...! Freydis ducked under Grimar's arm and ran back to the shoreline and into the arms of the sailors.

A sailor carried the hysterical girl back to the boat.

"Thorfinn..! Thorfinn..! Help us..! Help ..us!" screamed Freydis as she was dumped at the rear of the ship with other children wailing grief.

Mark and Peter took note of the repeated mention of Thorfinn and marched up to the Captain.

"Thorfinn?"

"It is a name. Grimar—come here and tell us about this Thorfinn. He is the one going to Vinland."

Grimar shuffled across the deck and put on his fake Christian sincerity.

"Thorfinn will be a warrior like his father and so will the men in that fiord. It will be the hardest one to take. We can't step foot on his farm. He won't listen. They will be waiting with weapons. I would say about ten armed men, and they are killers."

The Captain translated the words to Mark and Peter.

"Hmmn...some decent foes eh? We will take them," assured Mark.

Mark and Peter surveyed the next target and counted the number of people out waiting—three men, one woman, and a girl.

"Do you think we can get them while they are collecting bits of wood of the miserable looking beach, Peter?"

"Would be good. I really don't want another episode like the one we just had. And why was Grimar chasing a child anyway? We could have got her?"

"I think he his a pervert Peter, and that he wanted to rape the girl."

"That's disgusting. She is a child. I hate men like that, they aren't even real men anyway," grunted Peter in revulsion.

"He won't be staying in England long if he gets there. The Scots will be having him," smirked Mark, longing to see the sight.

"Do you think they will appreciate the gift Mark?"

"Yes they like a bit fun and as a good neighbour I share things with my neighbors over the border," mocked Mark with wide silly grin.

Grimar felt a rage boiling inside him. Quenching the rage proved hard, only the fear of the archers finally subdued it.

The next target was the last one before the ship entered deep into the Kangersuneq fiord.

People waved from the shoreline at the ship.

"Poor things must have been driven off course," remarked the man to his sister in law as his side.

"I wonder if we can persuade them to take us? There is only you, me, your daughter, and my son. Surely they would accept some furs as payment for passage to Iceland? That is where they must be from. There is nothing for us here now. And the winter could be as bad as the last one?" suggested the woman in her mid-twenties who had grown old before her time.

"I was thinking the same thing. And your boy and I can help the crew. We are skilled sailors and they maybe short of crew which is why they ended up here."

The prospect of leaving Greenland created hope and silenced all nagging questions concerning the ship sailing into the fiord.

The boat was lowered. Grimar, Mark, Peter, and two sailors scaled down the rope ladder into the boat.

"Are you off course?" called out the man from the shoreline.

Grimar, was thrown off guard, none of their previous victims had asked such a question. Being able to think quickly he opted to go along with their silly assumption.

"Yes...we are from Iceland. Lost some crew. Know any men who would wish to sail back to Iceland?"

"There you are I told you they were short of crew and that is why they wound up here. Why else would they come?" said the man with confidence.

The children ran on to the gray dim barren beach.

"A ship?" shouted the boy.

"Driven off course, boy," said the man sharply as he was anxious to gain passage out of Greenland before he faced another winter.

"I and the boy can both sail, if you will give passage to the girl and my sister-in-law. We lost five children, my wife, sister, and her husband last winter. We have furs to pay for passage," pleaded the man.

The Captain heard the man's desperate plea and was again glad the English archers didn't understand the Norse tongue. A mutiny was still a possibility.

Mark fortunately had made no attempt to read the body language and the tones of voices from the Greenlanders. The Captain did wonder why, but only for a moment.

"Indeed we can," assured Grimar.

Arrow heads stripped into the body of the man. Blood filled his eyes as he fell back on the pebbles. The woman convulsed before death claimed her.

Drops of blood crossed Greenland's crisp clear water. The drops became a stream. The ripples sucked up the blood and swept the stream over the wet stone and into the fiord.

Hysterical panic gave wings to the children's feet, but the steep diagonal rise soon took its toll on their weak and hungry bodies. The girl's cousin fell and was captured. Grimar lapsed into psychosis again, assuming he was protected his status as the Emissary's assistant, whilst the archers were busy elsewhere.

Grimar struck out after the girl. Empowered by sadistic lust his body was infused with frenzied energy. He scaled the step rise with ease and lunged forward, grabbing the child's ankle.

"I am going to skin you with my knife! Your parents called me Grimar the Fool...but you will not as your scream!" shrieked Grimar.

"Mercy! Mercy! Help!" The child's piteous cry was gathered by the wind and heard by Peter.

"Grimar is molesting another peasant child!" Peter shouted in disgust.

Oh what joy I will have with you," Grimar lay on his stomach. His his backside presented a tempting target for Peter's arrow. Only Grimar's usefulness saved his rump. Peter dispatched two arrows on either side of Grimar. The close proximity of the arrows caused Grimar's eyes to bulge in fear, and he jumped to his feet, grabbing the girl by her hair.

"You fool, you could have hit me, you English oaf!" Grimar charged down the hill. He dragged the child by her long brown hair behind him, her body bouncing over rough stony ground. He bared his teeth in aggression as he marched on carelessly down the hill. Grimar forgot he was confronting a warrior.

"Help, help...please!" cried the young girl. Tears washed her dirty face.

A disgusted sailor raced up the hill ahead of Peter. His muscular arm hit Grimar's forearm and made him whelp. The sailor scooped up the girl.

"We don't harm the children," stated the sailor, sharply looking down at the child.

Peter put his arm round Grimar's neck, pushed him slightly forward, and kicked his rump to send him rolling the slope. Stones bruised and cut Grimar's face. He landed in the cold water at the edge of the fiord. Reveling in Grimar's humiliation, the sailors and archers broke into unchecked laughter. Grimar knew he was once more the object of everyone's jest. Grimar incubated his hate. Soon he would allow it to hatch.

Peter leisurely strolled down the slope and unleashed scathing scorn on Grimar, standing soaked at the water edge.

"You gutless wonder. Try that again and a arrow will be stuck in you! You are a shadow of a man, Not even that. Just dressed up pig dung disguised as a man. A wimp that couldn't fight a real man," then with one arm Peter lifted Grimar off of his feet and held him dangling in the air.

"No touching the children! St. Ann does not like it!"

The Emissary, although he couldn't understand English, did take note of the reference to Saint Ann. Peter had been chosen by the Saint for some future deed. It was impossible to rebuke him for merely roughing up Grimar, who had placed him in danger earlier. The red haired lout would have injured or killed him, had not Mark intervened. Personal injury to him was injury to the holy mission. Clearly he had been mistaken about Grimar's devotion. The man was a bit of an impediment. Once the mission was completed he would abandon Grimar.

Mangled as Grimar was with hate, to attempt any revenge on the ship would result in being marooned on Greenland, or drowned at sea. In Iceland however, where these men would be seen as strangers, he could have them accused of all kinds of barbarity—even heresy. How simple and marvelous it would be to watch Peter and Mark squirming at the stake while flames crackled at their feet.

"Grimar is man without skill and is very misguided to think he could hold the post of tax collector!" remarked the Captain.

Mark's expression conveyed disbelief. He had heard many draft ideas but Grimar's dream excelled all of them.

"I have met tax collectors, Captain."

"So have I. Devious, ruthless, educated, and coming from the minor nobility. The King wouldn't even bestow that position on me. My blood line would be too low! He has delusions of grandeur. And the Earl of the Orkneys won't be bestowing any lofty positions on him either. Which is where we are heading, not Iceland as you know. Me and my crew are tried of long voyages, and wish to make a new home in the Orkneys."

"Risking the sea is like risking life in battle there are only so many times it can be done, Captain your decision is a wise one."

The ship reached an outlaying farm at the edge of the Kangersuneq Fiord.

A man fished long the shoreline. His wife scoured for anything that looked useful. He came to an abrupt halt and glared at the ship in the distance.

"A damn Royal ship! I remember the last one. I was twelve at the time. Robbed us everything we had. Both my parents died that winter. And there it is back again! To take what little we have again! But not this time. Oh no not again. Wife get the children, we are off," yelled the man with scorn in his breath as he fiddled with a knife.

His wife hurried away. She was equally as anxious to escape a visit from the Royal ship as her husband. She returned with plies of furs, goods and their children.

"Quick into the boat let us escape the robbers!"

The family leaped into the boat. The boy hoisted the sail while his parents up their backs to the oars.

"Row! Row!" ordered the man to his wife. He spotted the ship gaining on them. Ice floated at the back of their boat.

"Never thought I would be glad to see an ice floe," remarked his wife looking nervously back at the ship.

"Perhaps we ought to consider joining Thorfinn. These damn ships are always going to be showing up to rob us and the weather is worse each year," said the man pushing back his loose blonde hair and trying to muster more strength to turn the oars.

The Captain was curious and turned to Mark.

"Are they hurrying to the gathering or running from us Mark,?" asked the Captain studying the fanatic rowing.

"Wisely running from us," replied Mark. It was the best maneuver he had seen since undertaking this mission, he smiled for a moment.

"Grimar isn't going to fool those folk."

"They may go, and spread their good idea to others Mark,"

voiced the Captain with concern.

Before Mark could decide what to do, a fleet of kayaks, coupled of ice floes, proved a navigational nightmare.

The Emissary had no aspiration to endanger his personage just to catch stray heretics.

"Never mind Captain—we can get them later or those creatures with silly boats may get them. Sail on, let us not waste time chasing down pagans who are not likely to live long, once the rest are dead," ordered the Emissary in weary condescending tone.

The Captain actually had no intention of trying to guide his ship through the shifting path of ice floes, in order snuff out the lives of two Greenlanders attired in skins.

"Well wife what to do think of that? The robbing ship got rid of the Skraeling. And Skraeling and ice floes got rid of the robing ship. It is sign for us to abandon the boat and go overland to join Thorfinn. Damn the church for interfering with people's business and their foul greed and that dung pile the King of Norway. So there are Skraeling in Vinland—they are here too. We are off to Vinland!" growled the man. When he reached the shoreline his legs pounded the ground, with his family trailing behind him.

The Kangersuneq Fiord church stood overlooking the fiord and the people had gathered round the wharf just below.

Everyone smiled and murmured agreement. Children went wild and jumped up and down. Excitement exploded near the church half way up the Kangersuneq Fiord.

The Emissary wasn't too happy to see the number waiting at the wharf, in front of the church. He had asked them to go to the church. But the main cause of his displeasure was the wharf. Weather beaten and rarely used, the loose planks on the wharf could give way and send him crashing into the cold sea.

It was further proof that the people here were pagans else they would take more care for the wharf that led to the church. The Emissary strutted off the ship in a manner that would have put Mark's former lord to shame. The King of England couldn't have given a better performance. The twist of his wrist as he held his arm up, coupled with haughty display of raising his head like a noble impressed Mark too. He had to admit the man was a sneaky rat.

Eric hid behind the rocks. He was alarmed by the sight of long bows on the shoulders of the muscular men. The bows were taller than the men. How could they fire such a giant bow? The drawstring on the bow would take enormous strength to pull it back. Why did the leader in black attire need such body guards? Eric sensed it was a facade the men weren't there to guard the leader—they had come to kill.

Peter's instincts told him he was being watched. He focused his attention on the mound of rocks, which was the only hiding place worth having in the region. It was the place he would choose if he wanted to spy on an enemy. Eric froze. A man who held the skill of an Inuit and a Viking combined was looking for him.

Eric relaxed just a faction, he had never felt so afraid in his life and nobody had even done anything yet. Was he imaging dark forces at play?

"We are being watched Mark," advised Peter.

"Probably one of the natives, Peter. They don't like these folk."

"Could be," Peter turned his back to watch the Emissary.

"Good people, please gather at the church—there all will be revealed. Children are welcome to come aboard. Indeed we need them to come for the head count. The Captain has corrected me on how much room he has. Another ship which is about a day's sail behind will take those who wish to go to Vinland. Please, I ask you once more to get to the church," the Emissary's voice sounded like gentle pleading.

"All the children are here, and would love to go on the ship," shouted a woman with merry laughter.

"March in orderly fashion on to the ship. The Captain is very strict and obey him at all times," order the Emissary who viewed the children as heretic-spawn, and he pledged to drown them once the ship reached Iceland.

Ten pair of eyes filled with excitement. The children responded well to the command. Quietly the children formed a line and walked with great dignity onto the ship. The crowd of adults dispersed and strolled up the sloping ground to the church.

The Emissary walked in their wake. Soon the heretics who threatened to tear at the heart of Mother Church would lay on the cold stone floor in house of the one true God. He estimated the heretics numbered seventy, so a third of this nest of devil's would join Satan in the fires of hell. It was pity he hadn't brought more hemlock. But Grimar warned him the people living in Lysu Fiord wouldn't gather in a church. The Emissary concluded they had to be the worst heretics, most likely the one's who had instigated the rebirth of the Norse Gods and thus were unable to set foot on holy ground. It puzzled him for a moment why the people in this fiord were quiet happy to enter God's house. Then it hit him. The church had been defiled by pagan rites. That was why the heretics had no fear of stepping on holy ground.

The Emissary turned his head to see if his barrel of poisoned wine on its way to the church. To his utmost delight sailors were rolling the barrel up the slope. The precious barrel almost collided with a boulder. The Embassy was breathless the contents could have been spilled. The sailors pulled the barrel back and directed the object on it's path. The Emissary didn't take his eyes off his treasured object, and hurried to catch up with the delinquent sailors, it case they allowed real damage to occur. He sighed when the barrel was carried into the church and placed by the altar. The Emissary gave a short service and unconsecrated the church, in order kill the heretics. He couldn't dispose of them on holy ground.

Grimar strolled up the path to the church. No one recognized him he had never visited this fiord, but ugly words were spoken by these people, and they no doubt spent many a long winters' day, laughing at the saga of Grimar the Fool. He heard a few snorts of laughter as he watched the last one hurry to his death. Hopefully some of them weren't going to die quickly, so he could have a bit of fun. It has been so boring on the ship being subjected to prayer, sermons, and sailor's talk. The later as least had been a bit more bearable. He ached to rid himself of the pious Emissary.

If he joined the church as was going to have to endure more self-righteous piety? Was it worth it? Certainly the inquisition offered a man plenty of fun and power. But the training to get the post—that was a bucket of boredom. Then a brilliant idea formed in Grimar's mind. He could fake being a churchman. He could have all the power and fun, minus the boredom. Hearing the Emissary whine during the voyage was an ordeal which filled Grimar with the desire to 'accidentally' shove the pest over board.

People stood patiently inside the church. They had waited sixteen years for this relief ship to arrive and transport them out of the frozen wasteland. Expressions of peace and hope bloomed on their tired faces. Their God had kept faith with them, as they had with him.

"Our children are going to live," whispered one woman with uncompromising faith.

"I shall not be giving a sermon," announced the Emissary as he walked down the aisle.

Grimar stood at back of the church. He didn't want to impede the massacre caused by drinking the poison wine.

The Embassy notice the glow on Grimar's face, he was the only faithful son of Mother Church in what was once the house of God. The West Settlement folk just appeared to be anxious to learn what they could get, unlike Grimar. He was little ashamed that he had to deceived Grimar. Poor Grimar didn't even know the rules of the church. Then the Emissary recalled the danger Grimar had placed him in and lost his pity.

People lined up to sip the wine that was the blood of Christ. Each person found the taste horrible but not a single complaint was voiced. Grimar braced himself at the back of the church to watch the congregation slowly die. He was slow to fathom the impossibility of him being able to witness the act without endangering his own life. It was only when the Emissary had administered half of his poison that Grimar woke up to the fact. The noises in his head were growing, urging him to torture the innocent. He had to satisfy those voices soon before they consumed him. Perhaps one or two would escape and then he could quench his thirst for pain. When the last person took a gulp of wine the Emissary finally spoke.

"I will go now. Please talk among yourselves and I will return later but remember—only half of you can go to Iceland with us. The rest of you will have to wait for the second ship," lied the Emissary, well pleased with himself at having deceived the foul heretics. After this act on the behalf of Mother Church, he should have a guarantee of a promotion.

Eric gripped his bow. There was no doubt the archers had come to kill his neighbour. Deduction suggested he was powerless to save them either. His manhood demanded he put up a fight. How could he hide like a coward while they died? Because they had gone to a church none of the men would be armed. He had three arrows in his quiver and there were ten archers. Eric watched the ship's captain speak to one of the archers. The archer took aim at bird in flight, and the bird fell dead on the man's arrow. It was a shot Eric shamefully admitted no man in the Settlement could have made, not even Thorfinn. These archers could easily raid farm by farm and all the farms were so spread out. It was a very uncomfortable fact that he needed help to end the killer's rampage, before it took the lives of everyone in the Settlement. Eric barley held back his tears as he faced the cold hard realization he was going to have to sit back and watch his neighbors die. Thorfinn alone had the power to end the Royal ship's errand of death.

Inside the church people clutched at their throats and found their bodies felt as if they melted within away.

"Poison...we have been poisoned," groaned one man as he rolled on the church stone floor. People rolled on the floor their, eyes going back into their heads. Blood poured from their mouths. Pain began to leave the victims and a light was seen by them. A voice was heard.

"Your children will live, and you be avenged," cried a vision of a Viking of old.

The victims held out their dying arms to the vision.

One man grabbed a knife in his belt and with the last strength in him, forced opened the door and yelled loudly.

"Poison we have been poisoned!"

Mark ended his life with an arrow, out of mercy. He sneered as he looked at the state of the man's distorted and clouded skin. The man had earned respect by making an attack on Mark and his band. He was warrior and he had died like a warrior. His blood spurted out on to the Emissary's fine tunic. Revolted the Emissary drew back and stared in horror at his attire. Mark chuckled, he loved to see battle commanders who stayed in the background, get the fear of God put in them.

Eric in his hiding place was stunned. He had not expected to hear the cry of poison. He had to get to Thorfinn and fast. The Settlement had been made ready for battle. Screams came from the children, as bodies were lugged out of the church on the shoulders of the archers. Grimar pulled out the arrows, and then with a jolly cry kicked the bodies one by one into the fiord.

Children fought against the sailors as they tried desperately to leave the ship. But they were soon over powered and tied up.

"You'll make good Slaves," Grimar called out to the children in grim humor.

Eric was horrified. That is why the children had been allowed to live—they were to be sold as slaves. Eric was so shocked he found himself shaking. He held back his shock and reminded himself he wasn't a child as he had been in 1327, but a man, and the surviving children needed him to be a man, and a warrior.

"You are the spawn of heretics and should be glad you have been allowed live," shouted the Emissary cruelly at the children.

Heresy, so that was what this was all about. The most Christian folk in the entire Settlement had been judged without trial to be heretics. Eric denounced all Christian faith right then and there. Thorfinn was wise heading about to Vinland, far away from this evil church.

Death's veil hung over the Kangersuneq Fiord, the most loyal Christian place in the West Settlement, with bodies floating lifeless on the cold water's surface.

"This is Christian 'love'? These people were loyal and faithful to the Church and King, and this is their reward!" protested Eric to Greenland's barren hills. It blistered Eric's spirit he couldn't retire to his Inuit tribe with all the Norse in West Settlement in danger, even if they did despise and ridicule him. He alone could repeat the tale of Kangersuneq Fiord massacre. Thorfinn and Orm would believe him and act, but what of the people in the Pisigsarfix fiord? The ship was sure to raid that place next.

If he showed up at the Pisigsarfix Fiord in a kayak dressed like an Inuit, he would fail. They would dismiss any tale he told them. Eric entered a home. He found a Norse tunic which he put on, and then when down to the shoreline and grabbed a Norse boat with a sail. Now the he looked like Norseman. He might get the fools in the Pisigsarfix Fiord to go to arms. But first he would sail back down the fiord. Eric deemed it unlikely that the Royal ship had bothered to call in on the isolated farms in the upper fiord.

A young boy glared at the Emissary and screamed.

"Why?" he shouted.

"Heresy. All of you here are pagans, you worship the Norse Gods. You are lucky they weren't burn alive," said on sailor.

"You will be sold as slaves in England. You are the children of heretics," the Captain informed the children.

Grimar went back for his last dead body and found a woman still breathing, he was so happy.

"Oh..." the sound he made as he knelt beside was like a summer wind.

"Let's get you in the freezing water while you are alive," Grimar dragged her by her legs, laughing as she screamed in pain. His head bent back, and he sighed with ecstasy, with each scream that came from her dying lungs. Grimar dragged her to the water.

"Here we are at last. Look at the rest of them floating on the water. Now in you go..."

Grimar stopped and pouted. He stared at the dilated pupils looking up at him. The damn thing had gone and died on him,. She spoiled his fun by dying. He kicked her into the sea, and watched her body float to the surface. Grimar returned to the ship feeling refreshed. The sailors gulped as he passed them on the deck. The Royal ship set sail out of the fiord.

Eric took a boat with a sail from farm to farm, hoping to find someone alive. Empty homes were all he found, he cursed his foolishness. Time was going to be lost due to his folly.

The Pisigsarfix Fiord was soon reached by the ship. The captain counted the number of people gathered on the shoreline and recalled the number of people that lived in this fiord. He guessed that half of the population was on the stony beach. The people were waving and cheering.

The Emissary waved at them. The throng of thirteen children, eight women, and seventeen men stood by the rickety wharf and waited for the ship to dock near.

"Here it comes," shouted a man as he spotted the spectacle giant white square sail. It was the answer to his prayers; now his nine year old daughter would live. He looked down at her brown straggly brown hair which was the same color as her dead mother's hair.

"Those fools who left to join Thorfinn will be sorry now. Thorfinn may not want to go once he sees this fine ship," comment ed the man, enthralled with the ship's design.

"Look at the fine design...wow!" commented a young boy of twelve. A boat was lower and the Emissary was rowed to the shoreline.

"Welcome, we have waited so long for you," said the man of twenty six. He remembered the last ship and the horror of that visit, but chose to forget.

"I am not here to collect taxes or tithe!" announced the Emissary as he stepped on to the shoreline.

The applause of joy in answer to his declaration almost deafened him and demonstrated the people here were traitors and pagans. Else why would they be so joyful about not paying the King and his beloved Church?

"The King is closing down the Settlement. Ships can't sail here anymore, you will need relocate to Iceland"

More nosy cheers jarred the Emissary ears.

"Only half of the people of this fiord are here. The other very foolish half has gone to the Itivdlek Fiord to join Thorfinn on his futile voyage to Vinland. They will probably be returning soon when they learn of this glorious ship," chuckled the leading man in the fiord.

Riotous laughter came from the small crowd of people around him, praising their wisdom in refusing to go and seek passage on Thorfinn's ship to Vinland.

"Would the children like to visit the ship—we can send another boat—while I discuss business with the adults?" Suggested the Emissary, as this method had proven so good up to now.

"There is no need to send boats our boys can sail fish and hunt," assured the leader.

The boys waded into the cold water, helping the girls into the boats and rowed towards the ship. Then the Emissary wandered away without saying a word. That caused them to frown and wonder why. Seconds later Mark and his men unleashed ten arrows which all found their homes in their bodies. The survivors were momentarily shocked, and then before broke into a fanatic run.

The remainder of the men and women ran with formidable speed up the sloping ground. They were half way up the hill when the second volley of arrows hit the three men. Mark and Peter allowed the youngest archers standing by them at the edge of the water to take care of the remaining men.

One missed and only hit a man's arm. He fled out of sight. The youngest archer was mortified he had missed his target. The victim had somehow managed to run a good distance. Quickly he shrugged aside his error. The target had an arrow in his shoulder. He would soon die from the injury.

The injured youth divorced himself from his pain and pumped up his Viking spirit, to propel himself up the hill side and over rugged terrain. He had to reach men to get help. For a moment he pondered whether he should go south and try and reach Sandnes farm and warn Orm. Thorfinn and his men were better fighters however, and Thorfinn's farm was nearer.

The boys in the boats rowed frantically away from the ship, to a nearby cove. The children abandoned the boats and fled up the sloping ground.

"Get to Thorfinn!" yelled the eldest boy.

Mark and his men were too fast and too skilled at hunting down men for group of children to have any hope of out running them.

"Halt or we will fire, think of the girls!" You will live." yelled a sailor running up the hill in pursuit.

Sniffing back their defeat, the boys skidded to a halt on the side of the hill.

"Rolf has gotten away," hissed the eldest boy. "Thorfinn will save us," he repeated to his fellow captives.

"Murdering scum may you rot in hell!" he mumbled, full of shame and hate.

Mark and Peter didn't mind the emotional abuse. They admired it. The children had succeeded in making a colossal run, before being capture and still displayed courage.

The children were marched down the hill to the waiting ship.

"Twenty seven children," muttered the Captain distressed at the thought of having to deal with them. He wished to be rid of the children. He raised his eyes and prayed to Peter's Saint Ann for a safe and speedy voyage to the Orkneys, where he could retire.

The boys bent their heads. Tears of defeat and shame trickled down their faces. They were now the girls' only male protectors. The eldest boy whispered to the other children that Rolf had gotten away, and Thorfinn and his men who soon kill all the men on the ship.

Mark perceived that someone had gotten away by the way the children sat huddled together.

Mark guessed that Einar, who they rescued earlier, was equally as strong as the other boys and he would take him and his sister. To part a brother from his sister was cruel. He would find a way to influence the Emissary somehow. He had saved the sin-seller's life after all. The ship departed the Godthaab Fiord.

A gust of wind swept Eric down the Godthaab Fiord and then a fog hang over the Pisigsarfix Fiord, herding him right into the path of the Royal ship.

In utter desperation Eric silently called out to Thor. "I know have offended you Thor, but can you save me, so that I might save others?"

Eric knew fighting was a waste of time. The archers would have him shot dead in seconds. Quickly Eric made an assessment of the situation. The children who had been captured wouldn't know him. The East Settlement folk were noted to be good Christians, or at least he hoped they still enjoyed that reputation. Eric planned to pose as a sailor from the East Settlement lost at sea.

"Ahoy there! I am Eric Olavson from the East Settlement! I have been driven off course," shouted Eric, praying the Captain would swallow the story.

The Captain, knowing that gales were common along these shores, believed the tale.

"Come aboard, you will not far get in that boat."

Eric summoned up his courage and brought his boat alongside the killer ship and climbed aboard.

"Glad to see you. We men from the East Settlement are not too welcome here I can tell you. We fell out over trade. These people trade with the Skraeling!" he tried to put on a degrading tone as he spoke about the people of the West Settlement.

"Are you off course too?" asked Eric, knowing full well they weren't.

"No, we are on royal business. We aren't stopping in the East Settlement. Iceland is where we are heading to, after leaving here."

"I was going there too! I have no family. Do you want another sailor, and I can handle the sail," said Eric in all honesty.

"I don't doubt it, after a two hundred and fifty mile voyage in that boat," remarked the Captain with a smile.

The Captain's easy acceptance of his story convinced Eric that Thor was with him, and he opted to give him a second chance, for the sake of the children.

Eric noted the children didn't take him for a West Greenlander. Only Orm, Freda, and Thorfinn's people knew who he was, so he was safe. From the number of children huddled at the rear of the ship, Eric was shamefully aware he was too late to save the people of the Pisigsarfix Fiord. The people from the Pisigsarfix Fiord, who had gone to help Thorfinn with his ship building, were safe from the claws of the Royal ship. Then a strange sensation came over him...one man had got away. There was hope that the escapee may reach Thorfinn, and he might make a good old fashioned Viking raid on the ship.

***

The injured youth dragged his suffering body up the hill. He fought back the pain and forced his legs to carry him. Occasionally he stumbled, but the Viking blood that lay dormant for centuries awoke. He raced the top of the hill side, then slid on his backside did down the slope. He became dizzy, his vision blurred.

"Odin we must fight!" he cried out violently. Strength came to the youth's legs, he rose and strode on.

***

The children's presence on the ship caused Grimar to stare longing at them. The raw appetite to inflict pain was hard for him to control only the thought of sadistic pleasure kept his feelings hidden from the others. He could feel Mark's vision on his back waiting for him to turn round. The English archer already knew too much about him.

Einar also saw into Grimar's soul and shivered. Einar nudged Gunnhild and encouraged her to sing a hymn.

The Emissary murmured with approval. He nodded to Grimar.

"They are always singing hymns. I suppose there must be a few

Christians in the Settlement."

The words kindled deep discomfort in Grimar. He had to conduct a counter attack.

"They are probably the only ones, Emissary. After all if there were many Christians. They would have got rid of the pagans."

"Yes Grimar you are right, and if we do kill any Christians by accident, it will not matter for God will know them and they will have a quick entry into heaven," declared the Emissary.

Eric was glad he was leaning over the side when he heard the Emissary's statement and prayed to be saved from religious hypocrisy.

The ship sailed out of the Godthaab Fiord and away from all the tributing fiords and into the edge of the Itivdlek Fiord.

***

Astrid was regretting her foolish decision to come and live with her cousins. She would leave today. She would ask Orm to pardon her outburst, he was a good man and would forgive her. Astrid couldn't bear to stay with her cousins for another hour. Then she stopped, her two cousins were marching menacingly towards her.

"Astrid we have decided that you will marry Noddad, so we can go and live in Iceland for a while, before we head to Scotland. You can live with the Skraeling in Vinland," mocked her eldest cousin.

Unperturbed by the suggestion, Astrid calmly spoke to them in a reasonable manner.

"Thorfinn isn't going to alter his plans for his brother. I am of no use to you."

"He will change his plans and you will be Noddad's wife or maybe the Skraeling will kill him and you will become the wife of Skraeling living in Vinland...not your 'warm-island'. We will think of you when we walk the streets of London. Heh, I like the sound of that. Us living in London. We might even learn to read. We might wear good clothes while you wear filthy skins," mad shrill laughter escaped from his thin mouth.

"How do you plan on paying passage for a ship to get to Scotland, England, or anywhere cousins?"

Her mockery of their ideas angered them.

"I am going back to Sandnes farm," she turned on her heels and marched off down the hill.

Centuries of inbred madness awoke in her cousins and the two men ran after her in a frenzy. Astrid saw them and realized her foolish error. She ran for the boat on the stony shoreline. Terror pumped her legs as she raced down the hill side.

The two men raised their voices and howled as they gleefully toyed with their prey.

"We will have you Astrid, and you will bleed. You are going to Noddad in Vinland with the Skraeling. Yes oh yes," chanted her cousins, loving the chase and fear they had installed in Astrid. The madness was driving all reason from them.

"Oh mother help me! Thor help me!" cried Astrid to her long dead mother and Thor, as she faced the fact that without outside help, her life would end on the rocky terrain overlooking the fiord. The boat was just too far away for her to reach. Her lungs and legs were giving out under the strain.

Peter was standing on the deck studying his next target when he saw her, and the men behind her raising a whip. The girl was under attack, and it didn't look as if she could reach the boat lying on the pebble beach. Peter knew that was where she heading for. The girl could the one promised to him by Saint Ann, if so he had to save her.

Peter applied an arrow to his drawstring. The sailors, Captain, and the Emissary watched in wonder to see if Peter could hit a target at such an incredible distance. Grimar grunted, he deemed it to be an impossible shot. Angling the bow, the drawstring pinged as the arrow flew on it's deadly flight.

Ingolf trembled backwards as the arrow tip pieced through his organs and the impact plunged him backwards, ending his life.

"Yes!" cheers went up from the Captain and crew.

Grimar's jaw dropped. The man was a skilled killer—far more so than he was. Fear gnawed at Grimar. He could never take on this archer from England.

The other cousin tried to grab Astrid to use her as a shield, but Astrid pulled away and tumbled down the hill .She strove to untangle her stumbling feet, digging her heels into the ground. Astrid tried to use her arms to prevent injury, but to no avail. Astrid's head collided with the rocks. The image of a ship on the water became blurred, then darkness enclosed her and she lost her struggle to remain conscious.

Peter was furious. The girl could be the one St. Ann had promised him. He rattled in anger and sent another arrow flying into the man's hand. It took barely seconds for him to scale the rope ladder, and then he rowed ashore.

Peter then raced up the hill to where his victim was impaled. Ingolf gazed in horror at the foe coming for him. His madness gave him strength though, and he ripped the arrow from his hand, and stood with whip in hand to face his foe. Peter just laughed at him.

"You puny Greenlander, you think you can harm me that!"

Ingolf swished the whip around in an effort to frighten Peter.

"I am man gutless maggot, not a girl-child."

Peter barely bothered to exercise much effort dodging Ingolf. He grabbed Ingolf's wrist, wrapping the whip around Ingolf's neck and leisurely dragged him off down the slope.

Ingolf's eyes bulged, his face turned purple and his tongue shot from his mouth. His lungs screamed for air. His legs began to twitch. Peter hauled him up by his neck and dipped in and out the cold sea. While Ingolf was still alive, Peter released him and then sliced him open from groin to gullet.

"Pray for death," said Peter without pity.

Grimar knew the farm belonged to his uncle and the two men were most likely his cousins. The female was a mystery. One of them could have married. That would explain her being there. She could also be his uncle's daughter. Anyway it didn't matter she would be dead in a few minutes. Why hadn't the archer killed her?

Mark sighed he turned to the Captain and shook his head, slowly twisting his lips to one side.

"He thinks she might be the promised one, Captain."

The Captain's mouth opened wide, and he took in some deeps breaths. Peter thought that female was his chosen one.

The clouds above separated and sent a diagonal ray of light down on to Astrid. The Emissary gulped. The girl on the slope was being blessed by Saint Ann. Peter the archer and the female had found favor with God. Now he saw the reason for these particular archers being chosen. God had some great plan unbeknown to mortal men.

Peter ran to where Astrid lay and scooped her up, tenderly carried her back to the boat. Mark was alarmed that his friend was going to be lumbered with useless wench that couldn't even speak English. Astrid was placed in the boat, and Peter rowed back to the ship. Peter hoisted Astrid over his board shoulders and made his way up the rope ladder. Mark helped get her on-board.

"Is she alive?" called out Mark hoping the female was near death.

"Yes she is fine, Mark," said Peter happily.

Pity thought Mark, his poor friend intended to marry this wench from Greenland. A girl with no dowry, no skill and unable to speak English—what use was she? There was hope she may yet die.

The Emissary came forward and spotted the ivory cross dangling from her neck.

"She is a Christian." St. Ann has given us two signs," he proclaimed loudly.

The Captain deemed the Emissary to be as mad as Peter. Nevertheless the pronouncement was going to allow the female to live. He spoke in English to the archers.

"The Emissary has seen the cross and remembers Peter's holy message in the church. This female has been ordained by St. Ann to be Peter's wife," the Captain was of the opinion the King couldn't have better court jesters than Peter and the Emissary. He was going to enjoy reliving this funny tale for the rest of his life.

Peter looked down on Astrid's unconscious body as if he had been given a grand prize.

"St. Ann has always done it for me."

Grimar's paused for a moment. The sliver blonde hair, the eyes, nose, and mouth were the same features on Ingrid the witch. This female the prattling priest had spared was the daughter of Ingrid the famous witch of the West Settlement. His mind traced the family history. Her husband's sister had married his Uncle. Which would explain why the female was here at the farm. Grimar had to turn away to prevent himself from laughing. Saint Ann and the Emissary had delivered the archer a wife whose mother was a witch. Looking at the Emissary's holy expression Grimar did not bother to explain.

Astrid began to stir, she could see the shapes of men hovering over her. Who were they and where was she?

"Who are you?" asked the Emissary kindly.

"I… don't know. And where am I?" panic took hold of Astrid as she tried to rise.

The Captain translated her words to Mark and Peter.

"We have seen it before in battle. She has hit her head. She may remember in time and then she may not," replied Mark. His words were translated to the Emissary. Grimar was pleased she had no memory and wouldn't be able to express any opinions about him— that is if she knew about him? She very young and could have only been a baby when he left Greenland.

The Emissary studied the matter with cold eyes and decided he had no option but to obey the will of a Saint. His mission would be cursed by Saint Ann if he flaunted her will. The female was clearly a Christian, and as a mere woman, she wasn't in any position to oppose pagans in the community. It must have been dreadful for her, living among pagans and fearing for her soul. Could that have been the reason why she was attacked? The fact Astrid was barely conscious didn't bother the Emissary; a Saint had decreed the marriage and he had to obey with speed. At the very least he would be subjected to a rough sea voyage if he failed to comply. He trembled at the very thought of invoking the wrath of Saint Ann.

"Do you Peter, take this woman to be your wife?" asked the Emissary, the Captain stood at his side and translated the words.

"I do."

The Emissary uttered some words in Latin over the top of three of Astrid's finger and placed a copper ring on her as he smiled at Peter and Astrid.

"Young woman, this is your husband, Peter. He is from England you have only just been married," said the Emissary as if he were doing a great kindness. The Captain realized the Emissary had performed a marriage. Arranged marriages were common so the Captain thought nothing was odd.

Peter was overjoyed with his new wife and was beaming from ear to ear. Mark resigned himself to accepting the female as Peter's wife. There was nothing else to do. The sin-seller had just married them and that was the end. Poor Peter, he hoped the female was going to be a good wife to him. By the looks of her she had nothing much to offer, and she didn't even speak English. St. Ann hadn't saved Peter, the Saint had saved the girl. She was likely to be the only adult survivor in the Settlement. Mark judged her to be about fifteen or sixteen, with good strong bones and quite pretty. But that was all he could see to recommend her. Still, there was a thin hope she might yet die.

Eric was aghast to witness the girl's marriage to Peter. She was barely conscious and didn't know her own name. Were all the marriages in civilization conducted like this one? Then he began to think and remembered seeing her before. This was Astrid, daughter of Ingrid the Wise. Thor had granted Astrid's miracle. Eric gazed out to sea and pledged himself to Thor. Eric began to recall Thorfinn informing him of Ingrid's prophesies: A Viking raid, Astrid marrying a man who was the replica of Einar of the Orkneys, both in blood and way....

Eric surveyed Astrid again and the implications of Ingrid's prophesy. Astrid's incredible request had been granted by Thor, therefore Astrid must possess her mother's gift. The man who had saved her must be a descendant of Einar of the Orkneys. No other man would meet with Thor's approval. Eric's soul was shaken to the core. He decided not to try and reason out Thor's plans, but instead to go along with ride. He, who had planned to return to the Inuit, was now plunged into danger and mystery, due to his challenging Thor. He wouldn't be making that error again.

Astrid, still in a state of confusion and shock, concluded that she must have married the man before stepping on to the ship but hadn't long been married. He did seem to care for her. His friends were most welcoming. But she had no recollection of her husband. She had no recollection of anyone, just imagines popping into her mind. The terrain which surrounded the fiord looked very forbidding.

"Umm...do I live here...?" she asked.

"No, you going to live in England it's a pretty land," said the Captain.

Astrid was very relieved to learn she didn't live in this horrid place. The cliffs were crusted with ice and made her blood run cold. Why her husband was here was mystery. She thought to ask for a moment. Then her head hurt again and she just wanted to rest. She could find out why later. Right now she wanted to sleep. It was so hard to think, her head pounded. Sleep was all she craved.

The children huddled together in the rear of the ship had been roused from their misery by all the noise on deck and stared at Astrid. As they lived in another fiord they had no idea who she was. Astrid, still in shock, hadn't notice the children or that they were bound.

Peter noticed her eyes becoming hazy and took her to the only quarters on the ship, the one reserved for the Emissary and the Captain. He placed Astrid on the bed and left her there. The Emissary had very nice sliver cup at the edge of his bed. Peter thought his wife would like that. It could go missing on the voyage. After all, the priest needed help to keep his vow of poverty, and the disappearance of the cup would go a long way to achieving that vow. Peter left Astrid alone to rest.

"She is still not too well from that head injury," he told his friends.

As they were battle hardened men they had seen such injuries before. Mark hoped Peter's new wife would never fully recover and regain back her memory. Not just for Peter's sake, but for her sake. There was nothing in Greenland worth remembering.

Eric was still coming to terms with the fact that Thor had sent a ship a long dangerous voyage to save Ingrid's daughter. Was Astrid all that special? Or was Thor saving the children of the Settlement. Thorfinn's ship wasn't capable to taking every child to Vinland. Thorfinn had once told him of what the runes said: "West and life for the young". Now Eric understood its cryptic message—the children were going to be saved. Thor was taking the children out of Greenland. No wonder he had been commanded to live in civilization after questioning Thor's might. Eric then began to think that perhaps Thor had some work for him in mind, and that was the reason he was on the ship. If Thor wanted him out the way he could simply drowned him. No, he was on this ship for a reason. "I wish you had chosen someone else Thor," thought Eric dismally.

"She is a poor prize," grunted Mark to the captain.

The Captain laughed and agreed. He told Eric what Mark had said. Eric's shocked reaction made the Captain laugh more.

"I see you agree."

Eric couldn't have disagreed more, he knew Peter was the one who had been given the grand prize and it wouldn't be long before he discovered, how great a dowry Astrid possessed. Thor and Astrid's new husband would take care of Astrid. His duty was to the children. He had to find a way to save them from a life of slavery. He did think of getting to Thorfinn or Orm and trying to take this ship. But the archers were so formidable. Men in Greenland had only ever fought Skraeling and even then only in small raids. These men were trained killers and their arms were rippled muscle. He wondered if he could even pull the draw string of one of those long bows. Eric strolled over to the captain.

"Captain, would you get one of the archers to lend me his bow just so I might see if I could pull the string?"

"I can ask."

The Captain went over to Mark with Eric's request.

Laughter erupted from Mark and his men.

"You have to train from the age of seven to pull the string of these bows. But he is welcome to try. If he succeeds he will be the first grown man to do so."

Captain waved at Eric to join the archers and Mark held out a bow with long thin grin on his face.

Eric asked Thor's blessing in silence as he took three strides and grasped the bow from Mark's hand. To their astonishment, Eric drew back the string to its fullest extent and fired.

"No man has ever done that before," whispered Peter. He suspected some dark magic in Eric. The archers' eyes rested on Eric, wary of his ability. Mark had already suspected Eric had odd talents and pondered no whether he ought to ask Eric to join him in the river boat business?

"Would he be a good sailor too, Captain?" asked Mark hopefully.

"He would have to be an excellent sailor to survive a 250 mile sea voyage in that miserable boat of his," conceded the Captain with admiration.

Mark hadn't seen Eric fight, but his instincts told him that the man was a warrior and a formidable sailor. But one of the crew had already consented to join him in the river boat business .

Ahead was the Itivdlek Fiord.

"There is a damn ice floe blocking entry to the Itivdlek Fiord, it moves every time the ship moves. Emissary, we will have to come back later. I can't risk the ship! We will head for the Lysu Fiord hopefully there are no ice floes blocking our path," the Captain was very adamant. The Emissary was too afraid to even attempt to question the Captain's judgment.

"Sandnes farm will be our next target. Grimar, I want you to go and met with your old friends in the Sandnes farm and tell them that the same tale we told the people in the Godthaab Fiord. I want to have a meeting at Pointed Rocks, the people living down the channel are able to get there. You will advise the headman that the women and children are to stay at the farm while the men discuss the King's wishes. You will have to stay in their company for a while Grimar."

"Somehow I will manage it, Emissary."

Eric's mind flew back to 1327 and a boy called Grimar, who tried to kill Fresh Water when he was a child. The man speaking was Grimar. It was the worst type of information to receive. One of their own was betraying them. Never in the history of the Settlement had such a thing happened. Why had Grimar acted in such way? True he had been called Grimar the Fool. But he had been called Eric the Skraeling and then Eric the Hermit. It didn't justify the deaths of very adult in the Settlement. Many of the adults who had harassed Grimar were long dead. If he could do nothing else he would end the life of Grimar at least. Eric became very worried when he witness Peter surveying the terrain ahead of the ship.

Peter seemed to be absorbed in the ripples on the fiord, the birds in the air, which way the wind was blowing, the slope of the land, the rocks, the grass, and almost everything. His plan to sneak away and warn Orm or Thorfinn about the Royal ship was never going to succeed with that man about. Eric doubted that even White Cloud could match the man. Who would have thought that a civilized land such as England could produce the likes of him. Eric was filled with regret that he had ever stepped on the deck of this ship.

***

The news of a royal ship coming up the fiord, given by a passing fishing boat filled Orm with grave trepidation. Its intent could only be to steal the merge resources left in the Settlement. The terrible fact caused Orm the headman to relive the events of 1327, while he sipped the contents of his cup. There was no other reason for the ship's visit. Charity wasn't in the heart of Norway's King or its

Church.

He gazed at his barren home. All it had was a table and few platforms on the floor of the once great hall. The outer building of Sandnes farm was a shadow of its former self. The farm had little to give in 1327 and it had nothing to give in 1342. Orm at thirty three was the eldest man in the Settlement. he didn't mind dying as long as he left this world in dignity. He looked at his father's sword hanging on the wall. Orm vowed he wouldn't dishonor the sword handed down to him. He pledge to fight and die fighting, rather than allow one fur to leave the house.

"A Royal ship...not those thieves again," he groaned in disbelief. He looked at the slope, his aching body needed to climb. Orm grumbled again and walk up the slope.

His wife and his four men were taken back by Orm's fearful expression. Orm had a reputation for patience and wisdom. The men and his wife gathered something serious had occurred.

"The fishing boat that passed by said they are back!" he shouted.

His wife and four men with her exchanged puzzled looks.

"Who is back, husband?" asked his wife gently.

"The Royal ship, it's sailing up the fiord as we speak," shouted Orm in exasperation.

Jaws dropped and not one puff of breath escaped from the men and Orm's wife.

"A Royal ship," stuttered Freda.

"Yes, come to rob gain. But no! Not this time!" vowed Orm, his fury mounting by the second. He paced and down mumbling and grumbling.

"Certainly we need a ship. After last winter we lost all our very young, and the women with child. Just not that one...or do we?" An idea formulated in Orm. A thin grin framed his board face.

The last Royal ship was well built and had a brilliant sail. The finest wooden planks, nails, and pitch graced the ship. It was far too good for the greedy King of Norway. The ship was definitely a suitable gift for the deserving people of the West Settlement. Orm's mouth stretched wide as a devilish plot was born in his mind. The men and his wife were amazed at his transformation.

"We are going to take the ship, men."

The scheme broke all boundaries of common scene, their thoughts and bodies froze. His wife was the first to thaw out and regain her senses.

"Piracy husband?"

"That barbaric lot stole our goods and the price is a ship! That ship!"

"Men! That Royal ship that has arrived is a much better ship that Thorfinn's don't you think?"

The four men agreed and ripped aloud with laughter.

They all conceded it was justice after the event in 1327. A fight had to be conducted, which pleased them immensely.

"We would have the King after us, husband," put forward Freda in frightened tone.

"The King of Norway isn't as powerful as he used to be. We'll sail it to another land not ruled by the king Norway. Scotland is the nearest land out of his reach. We dare go to the East Settlement or Iceland. A gigantic scheme had formed in Orm's mind and he wasn't going to let go of it.

"Less than thirty men manned the last ship. We can muster forty from this fiord and it is unlikely the men on that ship will be fighting warriors, just sailors, they may not even want to fight. We weren't ready the last time that is why they defeated our fathers, but not this time. We will be waiting for the tax collector and robbing priest and no simple sailors will be able to take us," vowed Orm, relishing the fight and taking the royal ship."

Silly Astrid had prayed for a ship to take her to a warm-island, and one had showed up to take him and his people to Scotland. It was a huge joke. Still he would forgive the silly young Astrid, and take her with them. Orm wasn't vindictive.

"Men, go and tell the neighbors to meet as planned at Pointed Rocks. The same place as before, this time for the good sport of a Viking raid! Boil up seal meat wife, we are going to need it on the voyage," Orm felt alive and well prepared for battle.

Eight year old Olaf with sunken eyes, thin limbs and a visible ribcage, gasped with joy at the news. Scotland, he could be a warrior there. He could see castles markets, and plenty of ships. Adventure, people, and a warmer land could be his. Hope filled his shattered heart and body.

"Oh father are we really going to live in Scotland?"

Orm gazed at his son's poor appearance. One more winter here would finish Olaf. The news of Scotland had brought life to his son's face and voice.

"That we are."

Orm's idea was beginning to brighten up everyone. His wife thought of Halfdan joining the church reforming it, and Olaf being a warrior and fighting off foes. Freda yearned to live in land where it wasn't dark all winter and to spend the rest of her days in a land with sunlight.

The visiting men rushed to embark on the mission, and to spread the news to their neighbors. They raced to the boats and pushed hard on the oars.

"Halfdan will love the idea of living in Scotland, but could he be a priest there?" remarked Olaf in a weak voice.

Orm was displeased with his son's notion of being a priest.

A priest wasn't the life he had in mind for his eldest son, and he fervently vowed not to offer any support. That idea had to be dealt a death blow. Halfdan was third best hunter and sailor in the Settlement, thanks to Thorfinn and the Inuit. Halfdan was suited to an outdoor life. Olaf was the one who needed to a easy indoor life.

Olaf shuffled out of the hall. His pale face and bony frame distressed his father and mother. That Royal ship was his youngest son's passage out of Greenland, and Orm was prepared to pay with his life for Olaf's passage to a warmer land.

Orm's plan was splintered when the Royal ship showed up ahead of time. He had to revise his plot quickly. Orm planned to tell them a gathering was happening at Pointed Rocks.

For Grimar it was the proudest event in his life as the ship anchored at Sandnes Farm.

Orm stood waiting to hear how much taxes and tithe the robbers were hoping to get. A small boat rowed to the shoreline. A man in the boat began to wave to Orm. He frowned and wondered what kind of trick the King was playing this time. Only the man who had waved to Orm got out of the boat. Orm glanced at the man's drab attire. The last King's official hadn't looked so poorly dressed. Though Orm did admit the man's attire was far better than his own.

"Orm? Don't you know me? It's me Grimar, old friend," cried Grimar stretching out his arms and hurrying towards Orm.

"Grimar..." gasped Orm in shock barely able to believe it was Grimar.

"Yes I am an errand man for the King. The ship hasn't come for payment, Orm. The King of 1327 died years ago."

Orm was too shocked at seeing Grimar to think of much at all. He shook his head and smiled at Grimar, who he deemed as an old friend and a West Greenlander.

"This is wonderful...you have come home, Grimar."

"Only for a time, Orm there is much to discuss and very little time."

"Come up to the house. We can talk there. What a sight for my old eyes. And you a King's man? No one will be calling you Grimar the Fool. More likely Grimar the Wise," chuckled Orm, lavishing his praise on Grimar, as the men walked together up the slope and passed the outer buildings of Sandnes farm.

"Still a bit of a fool doing the King's errands. It is not a high position and one I intend to drop Orm," Grimar acted out the part of a tired king's official with talent.

Freda came out to see the stranger with her husband. She sneered at the man.

"Freda, don't you recognized Grimar," laughed Orm.

Grimar the mad killer had come back to Greenland. Why had he undertaken a dangerous voyage to return to a land and people he hated? Grimar could read her face with ease. He was confident he could disable a stupid human obstacle like Freda, and flatten her ideas. He wasn't a boy anymore, but a man who had engaged in years of exploiting human weakness.

"I was ordered to come. I am sorry but Greenland just isn't as Green as the Orkneys or Scotland where I have been living," confessed Grimar with a reluctant sounding voice.

The mention of Scotland and the Orkneys unbalanced Freda's ability to sense the reason for Grimar's visit. Freda's spirit was leaving her. Seven of her children lay beneath Greenland's cold cruel soil. Last winter Olaf was between life and death, and had not fully recovered. The most essential requirement was to get her two sons out of Greenland. She was past thirty her, life was nearly done. Olaf was eight and Halfdan sixteen—they needed a better land. Eric the Red lost half of his first the fleet on the voyage here, that should have served as a warning. But their Vikings ancestors had only been stopped by the massive walls Constantinople, hordes of fighting men in Spain, and hordes of Skraeling in Vinland. Thorfinn and Eric the Hermit were modern Vikings, both of them knew it. Thorfinn would be flattered if she told him that. Eric the hopeful Inuit would be sick to his soul at the very thought of it. Freda bowed her head and begged to whatever God there was to take her life, but save her sons.

"Come inside Grimar and let us know why the Royal ship has come and what you have been doing over the years," invited Orm.

Grimar entered the home of the headman. The vilest tavern in Scotland would be considered grand compared to this place.

Orm sat down wearily. Grimar's smile never left his face as he gave his attention to his future victim.

"Now business first, Grimar. I have a duty to the people of the Settlement."

How like his father, he sounded. He would die like his father along with horrid Freda. The platform he sat on looked about a hundred years old, to Grimar.

"I too have my duty, Orm. An island has been found off of Vinland uninhabited by Skraeling. "

"Would be better than staying here," Orm admitted, though he couldn't recall any saga of Orm the Bold ,who sailed down the coast of Vinland, mentioning any islands like that.

"Those who don't wish to go there will be taken back to Iceland. The King realizes he can't get any taxes from people here and it is too costly to send ships here for goods, Orm. It is simply money Orm. Not kindness."

The "too costly to send ships" phrase rang an alarm bell in Orm's mind, coupled with the lack of a saga about these islands off the coast, and the generosity of the King's offer to take people to Iceland. Not just to the East Settlement even, but all the way to Iceland. Grimar was far too trusting and he certainly wasn't going to tell Grimar of his plan, to raid the ship. Taking the ship was still on Orm's agenda. Vinland was being offered by the King. Paying the cost for transporting people to Iceland, was another gift that was just too nice.

"So we got a new King."

"Oh the old one had been dead for years. The new King wants an empire stretching across from Norway to Vinland. Every king wants glory and this idea is a glory hunt, I have an Emissary with me," Grimar was aware he had to give plausible reason as to why the settlers here should buy the false news.

Orm didn't accept Grimar's ploy. The offer to take people to Iceland was not an act of glory, it was an act of charity. Grimar would not have volunteered to undertake a long dangerous out of concern for his old friends. Therefore he could have been duped by the Emissary. Orm had no intention of including Grimar at the meeting with the men of Lysu Fiord.

"It is a good offer and Vinland stirs many hearts here, but so does the prospect of returning to Iceland. I would say half would want Vinland and half Iceland. I haven't heard from the men in Kangersuneq Fiord or from Thorfinn. Wait till he learns that Grimar the Fool now had a high position at the King's court," commented Orm in praise of Grimar.

"Not true, I am but errand man."

Orm thought that was about right. His old friend was being used. Grimar had returned to try and save his people, but Grimar never was very bright and the King had used him. The new King sounded even more greedy and stupid than his father.

"What have you been doing all these years have you married, Grimar?"

"Yes I married a Scottish woman. I speak the language. She died. I have daughter Jean that is six years old. I live in the Orkneys. Not in Norway. Warmer than here. And it is really green," jested Grimar over the word green.

Grimar was proud of his deception, old Orm was so innocent and gullible. What a shock he was going to get when finally witnessed the real Grimar.

"The Emissary wants a meeting to be held at Pointed Rocks as it easy for everyone to get to, Orm."

"That can be arranged," assured Orm most willingly as he had planned a meeting there anyway.

"I will see you later, old friend I must get back to the ship. The ship's master is a fine man. The Emissary however doesn't converse with me very often. I must confess hardly know him at all and he doesn't treat me too well. But he is the King's Emissary and as I said I live in Orkneys. And am just an errand man."

The Emissary thought he was superior to a man who braved a dangerous voyage to assist his kin? It was Grimar who was the better man. Foolish as Grimar was, he was more honorable.

"It must be good to live the Orkneys Grimar, where Norse customs and language are still practiced?"

" Yes but I speak Scottish too. Scotland is only a six mile from the Orkneys. The Hebrides still speak our language too even though it belongs to Scotland now."

Scotland, the very land where they were thinking of going to had islands off the coast. They could go there. His friend Grimar knew the land and the language. Once the ship was taken, Grimar would realize how he had been used and he would come round and join them.

"I must go, Orm, the Emissary is a hard task master."

Grimar walked out of the farm house feeling rejuvenated. He

could smell the revenge that was to be his, after all these years. Orm and Freda would die horribly and their sons would too, and he would find a way to make sure they weren't sold with the chance to escape. Thorfinn's family would next.

Orm and Freda sat down together and talked at the old battered table.

"I feel he is being duped. The king comes not to rob but to offer. It is his offering that worries me. A new settlement in Vinland? Two large islands have supposed to have been found. Orm the Bold never reported them. And Erik the Red's brood didn't either. I am expected to believe that the King of Norway has better sailors, than the Vikings? I find that very hard to believe, Freda."

"The next offer is even more unbelievable. A charitable King, whose father robbed us? Who has offered to transport all those who do not wish to go to Vinland to Iceland? Can you belief the kindness of our King," mocked Orm rising from his seat.

"Indeed not, Orm. But the ship is wonderful. Just what we wanted. Olaf and Halfdan sailing away with us to Scotland. Orm it is great."

Orm looked round his hall to see if he had any weapons. Freda smirked.

"Look what I found," from behind her back she produced a huge battle axe, and sword.

Orm rubbed his hands at the sight of the magnificent axe. He imagined splitting the Emissary's head open with it and watching his blood spurt out. Uninhabited islands off Vinland and free passage to Iceland—that King must think the ice had frozen their minds. They would be having free passage on the King's ship to Scotland.

Orm looked at Sandnes farm. The old farm was more worn out than his aching bones. The warm air of Scotland would do much to rid the ache in his bones. Greenland wasn't a home anymore, it was cage with strong lock on it. It could only be unlocked by a stout ship. He suddenly thought of Thorfinn, would he want to go to Vinland if he knew what they were planning? Probably he thought, the Itivdlek folk followed the Norse Gods. Scotland would not take kindly to views on that. He wished them well in Vinland. But the land wasn't for him and his family. They were just too European and too Christian.

Twenty children and thirty women arrived at the farm. They were to stay there while the men took the ship, then come and collect them.

Freda went into daze she looked across at the other women. Ingrid's words rang out across the years warning her not to trust Grimar. She joined her women friends in the great hall.

"Hallfred you are the youngest of us women. Take all the children except Olaf and go to Thorfinn. Tell them our men are preparing to take the Royal ship by force".

The other women frowned. Freda sought to pacify them.

"We must take all possible precautions. The children will be safe with Thorfinn if anything goes wrong."

The women very reluctantly agreed.

"Children go with Hallfred to the Itivdlek Fiord and Thorfinn's farm. Go now and quickly."

Twenty children followed Hallfred out the door to take a long walk to Thorfinn's farm.

Orm strolled down to the shoreline, happily swinging his huge axe and then climbed into his boat to row to Pointed Rocks.

"I don't care if I die this day, or even if my wife dies this day, as long as my sons live. God grant me that and allow me to die with honour, if nothing else," asked Orm.

As he rowed up the fiord memories of the past stirred him; the deaths of seven children, the dark winters, seal hunting with his friends, fighting with Skraeling. How Thorfinn could be friends with those savages was beyond him. Fresh Water was alright, but not the rest of them. Then Thorfinn would need to get on with savages living in Vinland, it was a most ridiculous dream. Perhaps he should make an effort to get Thorfinn to join them in sailing to Scotland. After they had taken the ship, he would approach Thorfinn and try to get him to see reason. The animals, he had forgotten about the animals, they couldn't take them on the ship with them. They would have to hold a big feast prior to leaving. What animals were left after that the darn Skraeling could have. Poor Grimar. He felt really sorry for him, but the man would come to realize that he had been fooled by the King and Church just like in 1327.

A boat floating in the water caused Orm to halt his rowing. There was no one in it. Something terrible must have happened. Judging the currents and distance, the boat must have come from the farm belonging to Astrid's cousins. However he couldn't put the plan in jeopardy because three people may have come to harm. Orm let the boat drift on.

He cheered up as he neared pointed rocks and saw his friends carrying a wonderful array of weapons. It was shame they had only two bows to take down the foe at distance though. The Greenlanders could shot down a target at thirty paces thought Orm proudly. Twelve of the King's sailors would be dead by the time a man could count to thirty. The King's sailors wouldn't be good archers. Axes were the only weapons that could do them harm.

"Orm, what a splendid axe you have there. Planning to do some chopping, eh," called out a man from his boat.

"I do—but not wood," laughed Orm.

"How do like my spear and you know how far I can throw this, Orm?"

Orm did and no sailor on that King's ship had a chance of being able to throw a spear as far as his friend.

"I hope I can do as well with my axe. But I don't think I will try and throw it."

The warmth of his friends made the fight so much easier, he hoped they wouldn't drift apart in Scotland. He began to think about what work they would do there? Sailing, they could use the ship to transport goods around the coast of Scotland. The thought of the King's ship not only providing them with transport out of Greenland, but a good living was hilarious to Orm. He would have to wait to sell his idea to the men. But he was sure they find it just a funny as he did. Orm thought taking the ship was justice and payment for all their suffering back in 1327.

"My father would be laughing in heaven," commented one man.

The idea of living and sailing to Scotland became a fever inside the men.

Kayaks were seen in the distance. If he never saw one of those boats again he would be very happy. No more ice floes and no more Skraeling. Orm looked down at his attire that was another thing he would have change in Scotland. The thick furs were coming with them to Scotland. He would never be able to get polar bear skin again. He hadn't asked Grimar how long his voyage had taken and what stores were needed. Like an idiot he had been thinking too far ahead. First he had to plan the voyage, and what was required for the voyage. He was getting away carried, like Astrid. The idea of living and sailing to Scotland had become an obsession.

Another boat appeared and the men gave a brief wave before they joined the gathering. Orm noted the serious expression of their faces. That is what he had to do get his mind on—the fight—and forget the rest. Thirty men wearing long cloaks to hide their weapons spread out along the shoreline to await the arrival of the Royal ship.

The magnificent wooden sculpture with it's stout towering mast and sail bellowing in the wind, took the breath away from Orm and his men. This was a well-built ship that could cope with a long voyage, and transport them to their new chosen home in Scotland,. It was well worth fighting for. Orm had to repress his urge to laugh as the ship mooring at the wharf. He had been worried that the ship might anchor out at sea and make their attack so much harder. Grimar had been right the Emissary was weak man. He wasn't going to come ashore in a boat as he might get his feet wet.

***

The vantage point chosen by Peter over looked the mass of armed men. Peter was occupied with the rocks and clump of weedy grass,in front of his hiding place. The gap just wide enough to him to look down on the any scene which satisfied him. It was an ideal hiding place. He lay on his stomach so as not to been seen. Peter's prime weapon was his ears and eyes.

The swords the men held seemed to have gathered rust. The spears made from rubbish with sharp ivory tips which almost made Peter choke with laughter.

"We'll take that ship," vowed one happy warrior pumping himself up for battle.

Peter regarded such emotional displays as dangerous. The mind needed quiet and calm to void haste and waste. He and Mark spend time doing and thinking of nothing before a battle. The men who had worked themselves into a frenzy faced defeat before a battle began.

"Look I can see that Royal ship coming, Orm," called out one of the group of forty men.

"Weapons behind your backs men, the two of you with bows go up the rise so you can fire down on the ship and give us cover," ordered Orm.

Peter was certain the hidden arms were going to create an impression on Mark, namely one that he was about to be attacked. A brief flash of pity for the ill-equipped hunter-gather warriors crept into Peter's mind, for they were about to face ten deadly archers. The Conceited simpletons and their glorious fearless leader, hadn't asked why the ship had come. Had they seriously asked that question, the answer would have arisen.

The ship drew into the flimsy wharf. The Emissary strutted to the ship's rail to issue a fake greeting.

"I am Orm the headman, I own Sandnes farm," announced Orm with pride.

The Emissary recalled a record about Orm's father and that death alone had prevented him being chained, and he was taken back to Norway for treason and heresy.

"Have you and the men decide on whether you wish to in Iceland or Vinland?" asked the Emissary in business voice.

The men edged their up behind Orm. Mark stood beside the Captain.

"They are going to be attacking, they want the ship. Keep well back," whispered Mark.

The Captain snapped up an intake of breath, before he could exhale, Orm gave the battle cry.

"Go!"

Nine men placed arrows into bow strings. Peter rose from his hiding place and fired two arrows, before the two archers on the hill side had even taken aim. Orm and his men were in too much of a battle frenzy to notice the men left on the hill, who they were relying on to help them, were already dead.

The men lunged forward waving axes, Orm slashing his rusty sword from side to side with vigor and fury. Nine English archers leaped from the shelter of the ship's rail. Arrows trembled and made tiny short whispering ping of music before taking flight on the breeze.

Orm and his men saw the agents of death a little too late. Orm gulped for moment in shame. Grimar must know he was a traitor. Sour shame was gathered in Orm, he begged his family to forgive his trusting folly. The terrible fate which awaited family and friends at Sandnes farm made guilt sank deeper into Orm, deeper than the sharp arrow in his body. Fresh Water would see Halfdan got to Thorfinn. But what of Olaf...would he die? Orm cursed himself for the disaster. His family and friends may die. Grimar had betrayed them, his wife was right about Grimar.

"Forgive me! Save our children! Let us not die in vain!" Orm cried to blue sky above.

He then worked himself into a berserk frenzy, snarling and yelling he charged forward. Orm swung his sword, which made it hard for arrow to penetrate this full frontal mode of attack.

A wooden shaft steel tip arrow zipped passed Orm's sword and into his chest, cutting though muscle tissue and into the lungs. Orm's frantic charge rendered him immune to the injuries. Air sipped away and drained blood. A second arrow entered his shoulder. Orm continued his charge and breeched the ship's defenses. His sword the sliced fingers of a sailor like shearing wool. He slashed the sailor with his sword and a fountain of blood splashed onto Orm's ash colored face. Then Orm fell backwards on to the deck in his death throes.

Eric holding a knife, pretended to attack Orm. "Olaf and the children will be saved," he whispered.

Orm looked into the face of Eric the Hermit. Eric had spoken the truth. Orm then saw the spirit of Orm the Bold coming to take him.

"Your sons live and will be free," was the voice Orm heard again. A glow came over Orm dying face. Mark bowed his head as sign of respect to the dying warrior.

Orm smiled as he gazed at the specter before he died.

Grimar was furious that his old foe had died in such a dignified manner. Eric rose, shrugged, and put away his knife.

Eric found comfort in the fact his old friend had died in peace. Thor would forgive Orm's folly with religion. He had died a warrior's death in defense of his people. Would he have succeeded if Grimar hadn't betrayed them? Eric doubted it. These archers were modern day Vikings.

Bodies littered the gray stony shoreline. Grimar saw a man twitching. He rushed over to the body.

"One of you is alive?" said Grimar. The man moved but no sound came out of his mouth.

"Let me dig your eyes out," hissed Grimar. He knelt down and he grinned as he drew the blade near to the man's eyes.

A voice boomed across the terrain Mark leaped over the gray soil. Mark knocked his hammer down on Grimar's weak wrist. Grimar yelped and was send backwards with a kick. Mark then grabbed his long hair and wound it round his hand, dragging him back into the litter of corpses.

"Now pull out the arrows and push the bodies in the water,"

ordered Mark, as he gave him a kick in the arse.

This was the second round of humiliation inflicted on his person. It was a greater than he had suffered as boy. Grimar's fingers became claws, his mouth opened with the appearance of snarling bear. Mark planted his legs aside and put his hand loosely on his hips and chuckled at Grimar's ridiculous attempt to intimidate him.

"The Scots and the French couldn't make me run. Do you think fake bit of manhood like you can?" jeered Mark.

Grimar didn't speak English but he could understand the body language. Moaning deep inside himself, he withdrew and went about the work the Captain had assigned him, disposing of the bodies. Grimar pulled out the arrows, licking the blood then kicked the corpse along into the fiord. Ripples of water sucked up the blood and red strained water flowed back and forth.

***

Halfdan cursed himself for being late to attend the gathering, all because of damn ice floes getting in his way. He tried to row past the aqua shaded ice mass but it floated directly into this path every time he sought to out maneuver the thing. God and all his saints must be laughing in heaven.

Halfdan jumped out of his boat. He raced round the tiny cove to join his father. When he reached the rise, he saw his friends laying on the ground with single arrow in each man. Halfdan's mind reeled. The Royal ship hadn't come to rob, it had come to kill. Halfdan ducked down behind rocks. He heard the sound of feet behind.

"Halfdan it's me...Fresh Water," whispered a voice rapidly from behind.

The presence of Fresh Water shook away some of Halfdan's terror away and brought his mind back self-control.

"Stay down Halfdan. Look to the rocks below. See hair."

"I don't see any hair."

Peter's ears had picked the sound of human chatter. Fresh Water took the chance of his life and rose to his feet, and waved happily at Peter. He pointed to the dead, grinned and nodded in approval.

"Ah they are your enemies eh?" smiled Peter and gave a friendly wave. He carried on down the slope to join his comrades.

One of Orm's men had escape the round of slaughter and reached a boat. Peter casually applied an arrow to his bow and then struck the man down at over two hundred paces. Halfdan gulped he had never witnessed shot like it. His tears formed in his eyes. Only Fresh Water's hand over his mouth prevented him from making a sound.

Halfdan's life depended on the expertise, skill, and character of his young Inuit friend. Something deep within Halfdan told him Fresh Water knew how and when to fight and that now was not the time.

Peter's ears pricked to sound a shuffled human foot. He whipped out an arrow from his quiver and placed it in the hemp draw string. Fresh Water and Halfdan stayed motionless. One tiny movement would be picked by this odd man who wasn't Norse. Men had died bravely down there, and to panic would be to insult the dead. Fresh Water and Halfdan remained calm. Peter relaxed and thought that it must the native who hated the dead men and re-joined his friends.

Eric however didn't relaxed. He studied the terrain. Halfdan's brief movement alerted Eric to his presence, and he had seen Fresh Water. He placed an arm diagonally across his chest. Fresh Water saw his friend and the signal from Eric. He left the ship and went to talk with the ship Captain. Fortunately for Eric, Peter was too busy talking to his friend. Eric had no idea who was on the mound with Fresh Water, but he would give the person as much information as he could. Eric joined the Captain and Mark.

"If they hadn't such primitive weapons those Greenlanders could have inflicted quite a few injuries before we got them," remarked Mark with admiration for their courage.

Eric asked with much casualness as he could muster.

"What is going to happen to the children now, Captain?"

The same as before, we are going to sell the children."

"I just wondered. I thought with the heretics in the other fiords all dead apart from the children, and now these heretics there might be a change of plans?"

"No… no. The children of this lot are all at Sandnes farm and we will pick them up when we will kill the heretic women. The children too would have been killed if those English archers hadn't made it plain they wouldn't put arrows in what they called 'peasant children'. Their lives will be no worse than here. The men are ex-serfs which is one jump up from a slave, trained to use those bows since the age of seven and have been fighting the Scots and the French. Peter's ancestor was a Viking, Einar of the Orkneys in fact."

"You are right Captain, all the men in this settlement wouldn't have been able to defeat these men. And that girl with the lost memory? Astrid, now married to one of the English archer Peter. That is very strange? That the Kangersuneq Fiord people were all poisoned except the children must have pleased the archers, they didn't have to do any fighting. To think if I hadn't been driven off from the East Settlement, I would have been home by now. But now I have to find a new home."

"Yes. I agree this is very confusing…, " complained the Captain who then turned round and walked slowly back down towards his ship.

Eric only had to go over the rise to join Fresh Water hiding on the hill. Or go to Vinland with Thorfinn. But Thor had put a curse on him and he was honour bound to sail with the children to the new world, and the way of life he hated so much. Eric placed an arm over his chest twice, he was bidding farewell to his Inuit friend.

Fresh Water bent his head at the sight. His friend and fellow Inuit was saying farewell forever. Silent tears fell from young Halfdan. Grief and shame fought a battle within him. He longed to reach his mother's side and fight to save her. But he was just one man and only Thorfinn and his men could hope defeat these murderers. Yet Eric's word rang in Halfdan's ears. Eric the Hermit was telling him that Thorfinn and his men couldn't save his mother and the children. The lives of his frail bother and the children of the West Settlement were in the hands of the only man who could aid them in any form, Eric the Hermit. Astrid had lost her memory and was married to an English archer, a descendant of Einar of the Orkneys. The old prophesy of Ingrid the wise had come to pass. Astrid had inherited her mother's gift. She was wounded at present, but what would occur when she was healed? Halfdan's mind wandered back to the spectacle just yards away.

Halfdan watched the bodies dragged across rough stony ground and pushed into the water. Grief's ugly burden was too great an encumbrance to allow Halfdan to move. Fresh Water once again placed a quick hand over his friend's mouth. Fresh Water knew they had to remain quiet and still until the men boarded the ship and it sailed well out of view.

Halfdan's grief and bitterness gave him great endurance and he covered the terrain quickly before he paddled the kayak to Thorfinn's farm.

***

At Sandnes farm, Freda waited and with other women. She wasn't overly anxious. The men outnumber the sailors, and she recalled the raid in 1327 had only been accomplished because they raided each farm separately. But now the men had formed a small army and were ready for battle and armed. This time things would be very different. She thought about how wonderful it would be to live in Scotland and use the ship for trade. What a marvelous life they would have. And the greedy King was too proud to even think that a bunch of backward souls in the West Settlement of Greenland could take his ship way from him. It was going to be a very long voyage of course. The ship dare not call in at Iceland. The ship had to sail all the way to Scotland. She and the women had boiled up plenty of seal meat for the voyage. No one had to go hungry. Once in Scotland she and the women would have to learn how to cook other foods. It would be a problem. Grimar was a worry, she still felt he was a walking demon in human form. She hoped she was wrong. As he spoke the language of Scotland that would be a major asset But if he was still the same Grimar, he would change sides as soon as he saw the battle start.

"Oh mother just think Scotland—warmer weather and beautiful court-side," uttered eight year old Olaf.

In the ripe fields of Scotland with better food, Olaf would put on weight and grow strong. Like his brother Halfdan. In Scotland Halfdan and his father would be reconciled. In a Christian land Orm would see the importance of Halfdan being able to read and knowing the ways of the church. She did hope however Halfdan would ditch his plan to join the church. He was a fine sailor and the ship could make them all rich. Halfdan had no idea what the church was really like. He hadn't even been born when the last priest stepped on to the West Settlement. That vile priest made many converting Thorfinn's Norse Gods. Generously, she thought may church have changed and become compassionate over the years, and had got rid of men like the priest that came in 1327.

Foots steps pounded the ground outside the headman's house. Freda and the women sighed with relief. The battle was over it had been won. It was time for them to sail to Scotland. Olaf mother's hoped Grimar was the person her husband thought he had become, a man with the knowledge of the language and customs of Scotland would be such an asset in the land.

"By the sounds of the feet most of our men alive, thanks be to God." Freda raced to open the door. Grimar burst in. The sight of Grimar brought a frown to the headman's wife. He was the last person she had expected see. Her husband had made it clear that he didn't fully trust Grimar. So why was he here and not one of Orm's men? Surely her husband couldn't have changed his mind so rapidly. Orm had never made careless rapid decisions. He would hardly do so, now.

"Quickly, the children must board the ship."

"Why?" she questioned bluntly with suspicious written in her eyes.

"Why! Because the ship has to sail now! There is another Royal ship. Surely you remember there was one the last time! If Orm had confided in me? I would have told him. And the men can't take that ship. We must get to the ship and sail. All the able bodied men are needed to sail the ship they can't come and chase after you," growled Grimar loudly. It was a superb lie. Grimar congratulated himself on coming up with it.

Grimar's plausible tale of events persuaded the women to act without further question. They didn't want their men to engage in another battle, when they could simply leave. And it had to be done fast with any other royal ship on the way. The headman's wife was in a quandary—was it possible now for them to be able sail to Scotland? The Royal ship might give chase. It certainly could alert other kingdoms to their crime. It was a mess. Grimar had a right to look furious. If they had trusted him, the men would have acted so differently.

"The children are not here, they have gone to the Itivdlek Fiord," said Freda, in a panic. She had been foolish, to send them there just because of her suspicions about Grimar. It was a jumbled mess, how were they going to reach the children and dodge the ship as well? Freda cursed her stupid hate of Grimar. It was the cause of their trouble.

"Come, you must all run as fast as you can to the ship. We can still pick the children up on the way," snapped Grimar hurrying everyone along.

Olaf yearned to show people he wasn't a frail sick boy, in need of constant care and ran out the door with the women. Grimar bolted the door behind him and chuckled away, as he leaned back on the platform seat waiting to hear the screams.

Revenge had finally arrived. His face was radiant, and he tuned his ears to receive the cries of denial as the women faced their fate.

Outside the women peered into the distance, they couldn't see anyone coming. Mark and the men came out from the cover of the outer buildings. The women's eyes registered horror and betrayal, but only for a moment. In twenty seconds it was all over. Freda was the only one who hadn't been killed outright.

She felt the weight of her folly and asked herself if she had killed Olaf with her idiocy?

Mark saw the single tear on her cheek as life began to leave her eyes. It wove a miraculous web round Mark. The icy killer bent down at her side. Freda's clawed fingers clutched his tunic. Her eyes held his gaze. He was totally lost in them. Sorrow laid its cold hands on Mark the killer, he tried to shake off them off, but it wrapped up Mark too tightly.

Freda extracted a vow from Mark.

"Save Olaf. Save Olaf," her voice wasn't a plea, but a command. She pointed to Olaf standing among the dead women, frozen in terror.

Mark knew she was instructed him to save a child named Olaf. Her ghost would haunt all his day if failed to do her bidding. Mark wasn't responding to fear, Freda had just bestowed her gift of compassion, on to a man who earned his living by murder.

"Olaf will be saved," vowed Mark nodding, his head over and over again.

There was a glow on Freda's weather beaten face as she nodded. Freda knew Halfdan was safe and now Olaf was safe too. She and Orm had been granted the one thing they desired above all else; that their sons lives.

The spirit of her husband walked towards her. He nodded his head and smiled. Their sons were going to live. She smiled and reached out for her husband's hand and died.

Grimar came up to him and laughed. "She is the headman's wife. The puny sick boy is her son."

The Captain appeared on the scene. He too was sickened and didn't want any more of these vile murders, for the sake of the Church.

"Grimar says the woman is the headman's wife and the sickly looking boy is her son," informed the Captain.

Mark's eerie feeling departed, but the cold hard killer had died with Freda. Mark sighed, why he had been so affected by the death of one older woman dying? He had seen so many women die, yet this one with her single tear, had extracted a vow from him. He was going to be hard pressed to grant the vow. Honour demanded that he did. Mark then realized that he couldn't engage in senseless warfare any more. He would fight to the death to defend his land, friends, and family, but no more would he roam aboard to fight for another Lord, King, or Church. Mark raised his head and noted that all the men, except for Grimar and the Emissary, shared his battle weary sentiments.

Olaf's legs wobbled, his head dropped to one side. All the women, including his mother, lay face up with arrows sticking from their chests. His mother eyes were wide open, staring up at the heavens, all the life was drained from them. He was alone standing among the dead. A scream that last at minute came from his throat. Olaf sank to his knees and wailed.

Mark stood over him and spoke.

"You will be lucky to last the winter. Still I will do what I can."

Olaf offered no resistance as Mark tucked him under his arm.

"You are a maggot..." snapped Olaf in squeaky voice.

"Boy, will have to learn to engage your mind. Then open your mouth. Not open your mouth before engaging your mind in thought," instructed Mark in response to Olaf's outburst without knowledge of what he said in Norse.

Dumped on the deck, black anger roared inside Olaf urging him to kill, but he knew he was too young and too weak. His hate would have to sleep a long time and awaken only when he was strong and wise.

He was on the deck of the ship his father had wanted to take. Olaf eyes stared at the sight of Astrid with one of the killers. The women of the Lysu Fiord were all dead. He growled at Astrid.

Venom escapee from Olaf's mouth and he roared.

"Traitor! Traitor! How could you lived in our house. My parents treated you with kindness and you cuddle up to their killers!" He pointed to Astrid. She walked over to Olaf, looked kindly down him, and patted his head.

"I don't know you. Peter is my husband," Astrid thought the boy had mistaken her for someone else.

The Captain was anxious to know about the girl and strode over to Olaf.

"You know her? We found her with head injury she has no memory boy, so who is she?"

"Head injury...you mean she doesn't know me?"

"No, she doesn't know you."

Olaf sobbed he was all alone. He knew none of the child captives. Astrid didn't know him either.

"She is Astrid. An orphan, she is sixteen can read the book of Saints."

Olaf's chaotic thoughts wove around Astrid. She had been granted her fantastic miracle. Could she be a witch, and the devil had saved her, and condemned them, because they were Christians?

The Captain strolled over to Peter.

"Your wife is called Astrid and she can read. She is sixteen."

"Can read?" replied Peter was wistfully amazed.

Astrid fainted. Mark inhaled—could it be that the useless skin dressed Greenlander was dying? Peter then could be free. Astrid stirred and came around. Mark groaned. He realized his hope was like wanting green grass in Greenland. Saint Ann's shrine wasn't being visited by him. The dithering sin-seller might believe Astrid was blessed, but he thought she was a curse. His disgust had come to boiling point, when he saw Grimar walk backward form her with fear in his eyes. The female was physically weak so why would any man be afraid of her? And Grimar must know her, but how could that be, Astrid was too young.

Mark shed any belief that Grimar was influenced by the sin-seller's pronouncement that she was blessed by silly Saint Ann. Grimar was too evil to be religious, so it had to be something else.

Mark's eyes shifted to Olaf, the only person who really knew the girl. Having come straight from a slaughter he wasn't a reliable source. Even battle hardened Peter had lost his logic and had the daft notion about finding wife in 'green-land' after coming straight from a battle. So what could he expect from a half dead boy captured in a massacre? He noted the hate building up in the boy. Mark strode over to Eric, nudged him and pointed to Olaf and Astrid. Olaf's snarling mouth and his eyes resting on Astrid alerted Eric to the impending disaster. Olaf hated Astrid. He took three long sharp strides and reached Olaf.

"What is wrong Olaf?"

"She is a witch she said a ship would come and take her to a warm-island, one has."

Eric sucked in his breath and was thankful the boy had spoken softly and the Emissary was at the other end of the ship. He had to snip these dangerous ideas out of the boy's head and implant new ones. Could he get Olaf to believe Astrid had been spared because of St. Ann's intervention? That was the Saint mentioned by the Captain. His minimal knowledge of Christianity had been gathered from Halfdan visits to the tribe.

Eric freely admitted he couldn't recalled the name of single Saint. Halfdan had rattled on about. St. Ann being an ideal candidate and it was the only one Eric knew of. Eric launched into a Christian sermon.

"Saint Ann has blessed her. This Astrid must have prayed to her. The man Peter had vision in a church. St. Ann sent him to her. Saint Ann is the reason. Trust in Saint Ann—look what she has done for Astrid? Follow Saint Ann. Astrid has no memory this must be Saint Ann's wish."

Olaf was physically weak and full of angst over the deaths of the women. Olaf began to pray to St. Ann.

Eric was thankful he had been able spin a better yarn than Halfdan. His gazed was transferred to Grimar.

Grimar unhappily harvested the apathy consuming the archers and sailors and Captain. The chief tormentor Thorfinn and Orm's oldest son were not among the dead. Somehow he had to rejuvenate the archers murderous zeal. Grimar was very worried. He rushed to the Emissary side.

"The main heretics are in the Itivdlek Fiord, just a short sail round the fiord and we can eliminate the last of the heretics, Emissary."

The Emissary's desperate wish was to leave Greenland. Personal comfort was luring him away from his dedication to Mother Church. A warm dry bed, good food, and above all the lure of dry firm land. If it was possible to achieve it with ease he would do it. The heretics could be left to the mercy of Greenland's climate on the western coast which seemed to be about to be imprisoned by ice floes. Grimar's devotion was also starting to concern him. Was it really his faith to Mother Church that was driving him on? Grimar wasn't going to push him to endure more of Greenland.

Mark grinned he knew that the sin-seller was tired like the rest of them. Dedication to Mother Church had plummeted, and Mark prayed it had plummeted enough to cancel anymore killings.

Grimar caught sight of the kayak paddling up the fiord, it had no difficulty darting pass the ice floe. But this stupid ship's master couldn't manage the feat. A common low dim wit Skraeling could beat him. Grimar contemplated on urging the Emissary to take the risk and journey up the fiord. He thought of black mail too, such as threating to inform the bishop of their slackness. He dismissed the idea. The terror on the Emissary's part told him that nothing would induce the pious priest to seek passage into the Itivdlek Fiord. Grimar comforted himself with the knowledge that Thorfinn's ship mightn't make it to Vinland, after all what kind of ship could he have built, and even if he was lucky enough to make it the Skraeling that lived there would kill him.

"Set sail, we are leaving Greenland," ordered the Captain he was more than sick of Greenland.

Eric was in nest of vipers, and knew, if he didn't take care, it would be a horrible death for him. That wasn't the problem. The problem was he wouldn't be able to help the children of the West Settlement. The ghosts of their parents cried out to him, to save their children. There were twenty eight children. The ship was heading for land he knew nothing about and was unlikely to give the mildest support to the children of 'heretics'.

***

Thorfinn was annoyed. He paced round the shoreline complaining.

"Why haven't any men shown up? Don't any of them want to take chance of getting out Greenland surely at least some would want to go? But one none of them do, are they stupid or just damn lazy? Every child under eight died here last year. Sure Vinland is at risk but so is staying here. If we can't live in Vinland we can build a better ship with the wood there and sail off again. Too much Christianity has led them to think God is going to save them. They are nearly as bad as strange as...Astrid with a ship, taking her to a 'warm-island'. Can't any men think or plan in this settlement? Fools, the ship is ready now. I will go and visit Orm and try and talk some sense into them. They can't stay here another winter. All the women who were with child last winter. Soon we will have no children. Greenland is dying. We have to leave," ranted Thorfinn in a fit of disbelief. Thorfinn decided to return to work to cure his bad mood.

Thorfinn and his men barley took any interest in the kayak paddling towards them, it was too far away. They were too busy loading the ship with barrels of cooked seal meat and water.

Thorfinn was still very infuriated that he hadn't received any word at all about who wished to sail with them to Vinland. Or if they had agreed to any of his suggestions, so now he was leaving. Even his closest friend Orm hadn't sent word. It was plain that the entire settlement thought their venture to Vinland was doomed to failure. The fools obviously planned to sail in their fishing vessels to the East Settlement and then to Iceland. It didn't occur to them that their puny boats had a good chance of ending up at the bottom of the sea. And considering they hadn't seen a ship in sixteen years the East Settlement would have hardly fared much better. Iceland itself might not be getting ships to visit its waters, either considering the change in the weather. Their hearts were wrapped up in European culture that they couldn't let it go. Should he wait one more day to see if the fools changed their minds? Thorfinn thoughts were tossing between anger and impatience. Noddad happened to gaze up at the hill and saw a youth falling and staggering about.

"Someone is injured, look over there! I will go and help him." Noddad ran toward the youth, thinking he had been attacked by a bear.

He reached the boys side. Barely unable to see and near to collapsing the youth spoke.

"Royal ship took children…the adults all dead..Pisigsarfix fiord, heresy…" the youth passed out.

Noddad was shocked, but his senses revived quickly, he put the youth over his broad shoulders and carried him down the hill to where the men were working.

"Thorfinn! Get to weapons! Get your weapons!" shouted Noddad.

Thorfinn and his men needed no second warning they grabbed their nearby weapons. Axes, swords, and spears were on display by the time Noddad reached them. The youth with the arrow buried deep in his shoulder, gave a clear message to the men.

The youth was placed tenderly on the ground the men gathered round him to hear what had happened.

"A Royal ship came said we were to go to Iceland then all the adults were shot with arrows. The children were taken on the ship. The archers had huge bow the like I have never seen and they fired one about every five seconds. I managed to reach the hill but even at that distance I was hit…" the youth passed out again.

Disgrace cast its shadow over Thorfinn. He had cursed the folly of men whose voices were now forever silent. Thorfinn asked the dead to pardon him. Precious friends lay in death's cruel embrace. The people from the Pisigsarfix Fiord, confronted the fact that had they not made the decision to join Thorfinn, they too would be among the dead.

Thorfinn and his men were jolted beyond belief at this news and when their wits returned, they pondered on what to do. The ship had to be heading for this fiord, but as there was an ice floe blocking the entrance at the present time. Thorfinn reasoned the ship would sail on to the Lysu fiord.

"Noddad come with me we have to warn our friends. And take that damn ship! We are going to take the children off that ship."

An explosion of revenge echoed from the men and weapons were waved in the air. The men were set to mount an attack.

A screaming of rage shattered the eardrums of the people gathered by the ship. Thorfinn and his people had never heard anything like it. All of them stared at the kayak as it came closer they saw it was Halfdan who was making the noise. Halfdan's face was etched in torment.

"We are too late," Thorfinn bent his head in shame.

"Murder! Murder!" shouted Halfdan.

Fresh Water slid out of the kayak. He had to support Halfdan from the kayak and keep arm round him as he staggered towards Thorfinn.

"Every adult in the Settlement is dead." The news almost incapacitated Thorfinn's group. It was a few moments before anyone found a voice. Thorfinn was the first to regain some measure of calm.

Halfdan then managed to be able to convey what had happened. "Fresh Water and I went Pointed Rocks. We arrived at Pointed Rocks and the fighting was almost over. One man tried to reach the boats and an arrow got him at great distance. Thanks to Fresh Water we were able to hide and still be near enough to listen to what they were saying. The Royal ship was hunting heretics. We were all heretics. The children have been rounded up to be sold as slaves. My father and all the men in Lysu Fiord died fighting and trying to take the ship. But the Church Emissary had employed archers with bows six foot high. Each one of those men shot an arrow very five seconds and they don't miss. My father died, holding that sword he kept on the wall. The archers shot all the women at Sandnes farm.

The people in Kangersuneq were poisoned at the church. Fresh Water and I had to watch, and heard all this from the rocks above. Eric the Hermit had somehow wrangled his way into getting them to accept him as a Christian. He talked to the ship's Captain. He knew we were watching and he tried to get a message to us. He made signs to Fresh Water saying that he would save the children. The children were only spared because the English archers refused to kill them."

Halfdan stopped for a moment and stared at the ground.

"Astrid is alive. She has lost her memory and is married to one of the English archers, a descendant of Einar of the Orkneys, remember Ingrid the wise, Thorfinn and what she said..."

Now Thorfinn knew why no one had send word. The voices of the West Settlement were blanketed in silence. The women hugged each other. Children stood wide eyed with blank expression on their young faces. Men tugged at their weapons.

Thorfinn was stunned that a ship could be sent over dangerous seas just to kill people the Church thought to be heretics.

"Our friends have killed by the Church. Those people along the Kangersuneq and Pisigsarfix Fiord were devout Christians unlike us," muttered Noddad, unable to comprehend the Christian religion.

"There is no way we can go to Europe. The church would be out to burn us alive. Nor can we stay here, they may send another ship. Vinland is the only home now," cried out Thorfinn in grief.

"To think murderous archers had more compassion than our damn Mother Church in Norway or our King. Foreign paid killers surpassed the Christian 'mercy of the Church," said Halfdan bitterly. His legs began to wobble, and men rushed to support him.

Agonizing indecision engulfed Thorfinn's mind. Honour and duty demanded he pursue the ship and rescue the children. To simply permit the murderers to escape was unthinkable. They could catch them out at sea and board the ship. He and his men were prepared for the English archers, while Orm and his men were not.

Fresh Water frowned he had witnessed the skill of the English archers. The Norse would be defeated by the warriors.

"The arrows would piece your bodies before reach the ship. Those men have seen battle many times. You have not seen it once. Trust Eric, he will save them and only he can. You see that driftwood up only the shoreline? The men with the long bow can hit that. Eric and Astrid will save the children."

Noddad felt his heart go cold. He had lost Astrid. She had chosen a murderer over him. Her love of a 'warm-land' had won out over her people's lives. The reason Astrid had married a foreigner was only to get to her precious new land. Astrid was   Loki's creature. Lost her memory—she had lost loyalty and love, that was what Astrid had lost, if she very really had any.

"I hope you die a horrid death Astrid", hissed Noddad. His curse flew on the cold winds of Greenland.

Thorfinn was shocked. Thor had granted Astrid's fantastic request. What Thor had bestowed on him and his people was small in comparison to what Thor had given to Astrid. Thorfinn was far too fearful of Thor's wrath to question the wisdom of the Norse Gods. Thor had some plan in mind for Astrid and her children. Yet Thorfinn found it near impossible to shake himself from the fact Thor has showered mercy and grace on Astrid. He was going to speak to Noddad about it later. But Thorfinn had more urgent matters to attend to and very little time to decide.

Thorfinn threw open his arms.

"Mighty Thor, Mighty Odin grant us wisdom. Do we fight of do we flee and trust Eric the Hermit to save the children of the West Settlement? Show us a sign. Our heats are torn Mighty Thor. Christian wolves have come among us. Friends are dead, our children to be sold as slaves."

Halfdan touched the rune pouch Astrid had given him.

"I have Astrid's runes, the ones given to her by her mother Ingrid."

"Let us consult the runes," said Thorfinn.

Halfdan asked how or who will save the children and then threw the runes.

"Odin's warrior in the West. Not Eric or Astrid."

Thorfinn licked his lips and pondered on the answer. "There must be some follower of Odin in Iceland for that is where the ship would be heading."

Thorfinn had to make the hardest decision of his life, did he try to take the ship, or leave the task to Thor and Eric, and one 'warrior in the West'? He looked at the women and children, if his men failed the women would be killed, and the children enslaved. He had to accept that all he could do was save the people here. The defeat was grinding down his manhood.

Tear stricken, people boarded the ship. Noddad cast his vision over the family farm that had been there for nearly three hundred years. The only home he ever known. The West Settlement was a home for ghosts. The places they visited and hunted were all empty now. He wondered what story the church would spin to the outside world. Would it tell the world the West Settlement was a home full of heretics or make up some another lie to explain, why no one lived here anymore? Noddad was sick with disappointment.

Then something appeared in the distance.

"Hold! Look! Look!" shouted Noddad.

Hallfred and the children marched over the terrain, waving and shouting.

Everyone on board the ship sobbed with joy, at the sight of the survivors. The children of the Lysu Fiord were alive and free. He thanked Thor for saving them, now he could help his dead friends, by caring for their children.

Noddad leapt over the ship rail, to meet the Lysu folk who walked merrily along. The smile on Hallfred's face told Noddad she didn't know what had happened.

"I am sorry to trouble you, but silly Freda doesn't trust Grimar and she told and me to bring the children in case something went… Oh no what has happened?" She cried.

Noddad led her and the children to the ship. Tearful women and angry men stood on the deck. The children were lifted on to the deck. When every child was aboard Thorfinn finally spoke.

"Your fathers are dead. Your fathers died fighting trying to save you, but they were out numbered. They would have won but for the church's betrayal. Foreign archers killed them. We have to sail to Vinland. You owe it to your parents to live or else they will have died in vain."

"Grimar! He was the one who betrayed them!" Hallfred yelled.

Thorfinn froze. Grimar had come back to Greenland. Loki's demon was loose on the West Settlement.

"Grimar told Orm that the King had found islands off the coast of Vinland that were uninhabited. And those who didn't want to go there could go to Iceland. Orm thought Grimar was an old friend returning home to try and save us. Orm distrusted the Church and King, but not with Grimar. He thought Grimar was being used by the King. Grimar's betrayal was why Orm and the men were defeated. Not those odd archers you speak of. It was Grimar. Grimar!" rallied Hallfred in rage.

Thorfinn wasn't going to argue with Hallfred. She was right only a Greenlander would know the layout of the Settlement, and be accepted so readily by the people, especially Orm. That demon had lured his fellow West Greenlanders to their deaths.

"Grimar. I remember him. He was a demon as a child. Eric the Hermit would remember him too. Grimar had tried to skin Fresh Water alive, he won't be able to fool Eric the Hermit," Thorfinn speculated Grimar would be facing his worst enemy, and one with remarkable patience.

"Eric is honorable he will save the children," interjected Fresh Water adamantly.

Thorfinn believed Eric was trying to dispose of Grimar, but he had no faith in Eric accomplishing the other feat. He didn't know enough about the land he was going to and Eric would be incarcerated in civilization. Eric the Hermit couldn't even withstand living in the Settlement. He would be on the brink of insanity in Iceland.

Halfdan also didn't have any confidence in Eric being able to function to any degree in a Christian land, let alone rescue children from the clutches of Mother Church. Eric was the last person who could manage such a marvel. Olaf's life and happiness was in the hands of Eric the Hermit. A man who hated the Norse Gods as much as he hated the Christians. Fortunately the runes foretold of a 'warrior in the west'. He would put his faith in what the runes said, not in Eric the hermit.

"We have to go, Olaf and the children are in Thor's hands," said Thorfinn firmly.

Halfdan noted Thorfinn thought nothing of providing for the twenty children. Neither did anyone on aboard the ship. Women rushed to comfort the grief stricken children. Hallfred was now immobilized too as she came to realize she was the only surviving adult female. If Freda hadn't been so suspicious of Grimar, she would be dead too. She was thankful all her family had died two years ago and she had no one left to mourn. Halfdan rushed to her side.

"Hallfred, we will be fine in Vinland."

Ice floes that caused distress in the past had on this occasion repelled an attack. People's lives could have been lost. Once again Thor had come to their aid. The horrid white pillars of doom were gone. The ship could now leave. Thorfinn walked over to Fresh Water.

"I wish White Cloud and all the Inuit well. Don't trust any Christians that show up. May Thor be with you and yours now and always my friend," uttered Thorfinn. He was proud to have known White Cloud and his people.

Thorfinn turned his mind to life in Vinland. He was armed with Orm the Bold's saga and a map. The worst part of the voyage would be crossing the sea between here and Vinland. Once there they could follow the coastline. A new world and a new life awaited them and he hoped that the old world wouldn't arrive, until the evil church had been annihilated. Halfdan gave his departing memorial service as the ship sailed into fiord. Everyone stood silenced and listened. Thorfinn was amazed the youth could find such words.

"Sorrow is West Greenland's crown. Shining, our tears are the jewels of disbelief which are laden on that crown. Children too would be among dead. But Foreign killers, these lowly men of a distant land, unbound by honor's decree, rose above the holy church, and said it cannot be.

Our children shackled in slavery will live free, by the sword of Odin's warrior, waiting on that far distant shore. And to our kin's children we say;

May grief not hound ye.
Nor hate and despair cage ye.
On that far distant shore.
May new homes be found, by ye.
On that far distant shore.
May ye find family and friends, loyal to the end.
On that far distant shore.
May ye live in green but never in greed.
On that far distant shore.
Astrid will wake.
On that far distant shore.
Eric and the paths he will take will shake that far distant shore.
Grimar we commend ye to Odin's kind care. On that far distant shore."

"We sail now for Vinland."

"We are leaving the fiords," announced Thorfinn.

Everyone watch in silence as the sail was snatched by the wind.

"Goodbye and good riddance," shouted Halfdan from the ship's rail. He was glad the ship didn't have to sail past Sandnes farm.

As the ship reached the edge of the fiord the people on the right side of the ship saw two bodies with arrows in their backs on the shoreline.

The farm belonged to Grimar's cousins apparently Grimar hadn't made any effort to save his own kin. Thorfinn looked again. One of them had whip in his hand. Maybe he had tried to defend himself.

Stands of long fair hair floated on the fiord, Halfdan sobbed and wondered who she might be, was her child on this ship?

The ship was under favorable winds and reached the Godthaab Fiord.

"We are almost out. Look up ahead. It is the Royal ship we couldn't catch them even if we tried. Grimar. If I had known he was among them I would have guessed the ship was up to no good. He must have been committing his sadistic acts wherever he lived before coming here. His madness eats him. Noddad, I would love to see what Odin's warrior does to him. Pity I won't see it. I won't ask Thor to sink that ship because our children are on it. Strange they are being taken to safety by people who hate them. I don't understand why those bowmen sought to spare the children. They certainly didn't care about the adults. There must be loads of wars going off in Europe to produce men like that. Perhaps they go and raid people just like the Vikings did. I am really puzzled by their actions. I should have listen when Ingrid told me 'Vikings would raid'. The men were modern Vikings".

I'll ask Halfdan to tell me more about it later. He is in no good state at the moment, Thorfinn."

"None of us are in very good state. Who would have thought of such thing? I didn't and you know how much I hate the church."

"We all do now. Halfdan most of all. We haven't lost anybody. He has lost everybody. Just like those children on the ship."

"I suppose Iceland will be their first port of call?" asked Noddad casually.

Thorfinn frowned. Icelandic people wouldn't be too pleased to hear of what had happened in Thorfinn's opinion. Selling the children there would be impossible there. Norway was too far. The Orkneys—that was where he thought the ship was heading. It was just off Scotland and if the children were sold in Scotland, no one would be able understand their language.

Thorfinn was filled with sadness again. He started blaming himself again. If he had worked a little harder the ship could have been finished by this time and at least his old friend Orm and his family would be sailing with him today, instead of being at the bottom of the fiord. It was his own laziness that had led to the death of his friend Orm. A man who had always thought of the settlement's need above his own needs, and was blessed with wisdom. If we have another son he will bear your name. If we have a daughter she shall be called Freda, vowed Thorfinn in silence.

Some of the men moved over to Thorfinn. They too were full of regret.

"If we had sent word bit earlier..." said one youth.

"I too thought that," confessed Thorfinn.

"To think not one person from Kangersuneq got away, not one. I would so happy to know one of them had gotten away. I would...." Noddad stopped in the middle of his sentence.

His eyes were on a boat. A small battered boat.

"We are from the Kangersuneq Fiord," cried out a man, at the oars.

Hailing shouts of joy erupted from the deck.

"Get on-board quick," ordered Thorfinn.

The man and his family were puzzled by the enormous welcome they had received. Once on deck Thorfinn enlightened the family to fate of their fellow West Greenlanders. The man was shaken by the knowledge. Only his suspicions had saved his family.

ESCAPE

Thor calmed the seas allowed his followers to reach the shores of Vinland. Cries of ecstatic joy sent the sea gulls flying high in the sky. Halfdan went down on bended knees in thanks to Thor for enabling them to escape. All the people on board went silent to give thanks to Thor.

Rolling forests of wood covered the landscape, with crowns of green gracing the branches, the sight made the hearts of the Greenlanders soar. They gripped their hands together and pressed them to their mouths in awe. Nature had lavished its bounty on this new land.

Thorfinn then decided to risk taking the route suggested by Halfdan. The youth's grandmother may have been a fraud, but if she was Abenaki her knowledge could save their lives. The ship reached the narrow channel described by her. No other record existed of this channel, because Halfdan's grandmother was Abenaki.

High cliffs flanked the narrow passage and the water was a raging torrent. Everyone on board was praying for a quick end. Thorfinn grinned and laughed loudly as the sea foam washed over his face, his Viking spirit reveled in the rough ride. His younger brother too was enjoying himself. The ship entered a calm gulf. Halfdan strolled over the deck to Thorfinn.

"There is a huge river to the west of where we are. The tribe up the river are very violent. The Maliseet live to the south, and further south by the sea live the East Abenaki," Halfdan informed Thorfinn.

"There is an island directly ahead. Let us go and see what is there. We can shelter the ship in the cove." Thorfinn was anxious to find a friendly tribe to accept them, as he knew that was there only chance of survival.

Thorfinn's people were driven off the island by a hail of arrows. Disappointment ripped into Thorfinn's plan. Was this the response he could except throughout Vinland? The ship sailed on.

Another island loomed in the distance. It had a safe cove to shelter the ship. Suddenly a pillar of smoke was spotted.

"It is an attack!" Thorfinn snapped.

"Half of you men, come with me, the rest stay on the ship. We are going to see if we can aid the victims!"

Six stout men armed with axes, bows, and spears leapt over the ship's side and into the sea. Thorfinn's sword gleamed in the sunlight and it sat lightly in his broad powerful hand. He and his men changed forward on a Viking raid as their ancestors had done eons ago.

***

Tall Tree and Blue Grass stood surrounded by the seven Mohawk warriors. Earlier in the day they and Owl Wing had been accused of witchcraft by the members of the tribe, who now laid scalped on the ground. The young powerful built warriors were determined to die fighting. They would not allow themselves to be tortured to death by the Mohawks. Owl Wing, a girl of 16 years was tied to a pole and brushwood was at her feet. She knew she couldn't bare the pain, and the Mohawk warriors would laugh at her screams.

Owl Wing envied Tall Tree and Blue Grass being able to die well. Four years ago the three of them had been taken captive by the Maliseet tribe and today they had been accused by the new shaman of being witches and were to killed when the Mohawks attacked.

Now she faced with death by burning.

Owl Wing's jaw fell, her pupils dilated, as out of the woods charged, pale skinned ugly hairy men. A bear fled in terror from the one armed with a shining weapon. Howls of horror bellowed from the throats of five Mohawks, as the bear fled. Two of the Mohawks turned to face Thorfinn and his men

Thorfinn sliced the head off of one of the Mohawk with single stoke of his sword. Blood made a stream on his steel blade. Noddad picked up the other Mohawk and spun him round by his ankles then banged his head into the rocks. The other five Mohawks just ran.

Thorfinn made a sign of friendship to Tall Tree and Blue Grass. Owl Wing was cut free by Noddad. Halfdan tossed his head toward Thorfinn. Naddod's intention towards Owl Wing was obvious to everyone.

"My bother, the ugly, hairy bearded one wants Owl Wing. Let us hope he takes her before he learns of her sharp tongue."

"Yes Blue Grass, I think he will. These are no spirits, they are men like us."

Owl Wing was a quick thinker and drew pictures in the dirt. Halfdan, having spent time with the Inuit understood the meaning very quickly. The talisman round his neck dropped in full view. Owl Wing instantly recognized it.

"Abenaki!" she pointed to herself and to Tall Tree and Blue Grass.

Halfdan turned to Thorfinn and beamed with relief and joy.

"They are not of this tribe, they are Abenaki. The girl indicates there is a small island not far from here where the Mohawks and Maliseet won't go. We could stay there until the spring and be safe."

"I have told the one I will name Without Fear, about the island where the Mohawks and Maliseet won't go. The young one is their shaman, he is Spirit Eyes. Hairy Bush likes me," Owl Wing informed them with her usual haughty voice.

Thorfinn looked round he hadn't succeeded in gaining a new home for his tribe, but he had gained two fine looking warriors who fought against seven men. The two warriors knew the land, its animals and its dangers. During the cooler weather ahead, the young warriors could teach them about the forest. Added to that was the fact his brother had found a wife, and Astrid would be forgotten. If they failed to find a home here in Vinland he would sail to the Hebrides near Scotland.

Now his people could rest and live on a small Island, in a safe place, enclosed from the open sea. They had escaped the church's wrath.

BOUND FOR THE ORKNEYS

Eric stood on the deck of the Royal ship, Iceland and the Faroes islands were far behind him. The Emissary had been given a bad welcome, and opted to leave very quickly. Eric was amused by the response of his Norse cousins, who apparently still held true to Norse customs.

Grimar's face went ash white when the Captain announced the ship was bound for the Orkneys. Eric assumed Grimar must know something about the place and took up a conversation with Loki's chief envoy, Grimar.

Happy to have company, Grimar embarked on long lecture of how the Earl of the Orkneys was prickly man with pride higher than any wave. He also told of how the Earl's father had lost lands in Scotland due to his siding with the English. To his surprise, Eric learnt that Scotland was only six miles away and that Scotland was an enemy of England and not too fond of the Orkneys. An escape route was available.

Grimar rattled on about how only Lords were allowed to hunt. Eric's Viking and Inuit spirit rebelled at that news. That the church allowed meat to be eaten only on certain days, dismayed him further. Eric immediately pulled himself together; his first obstacle was rescuing the children. Stealing a boat was an easy feat for an Inuit. The archers were all leaving the ship when it docked in the Orkneys as was the captain and the ship's crew. So the children maybe left unguarded for a brief time. Astrid caught his attention and Eric strolled over to her.

The daughter of Ingrid the Wise awoke and voice was so like her mother's before her.

"A warrior waits and fish. Go tell Mark you wish to work for him."

Thor had a warrior on the Orkneys, this was joyous news, but the fish was very puzzling however. Eric began to relax knowing that he had help in the Orkneys. Mark had offered him work on the boat he was buying, because Mark knew nothing about boats. The idea of life on a river boat appealed Eric and young Einar seemed to like the idea too. Olaf just rocked himself in the corner of the ship. Eric was shocked, Orm's spirit hadn't stir in the boy nor had Freda's dignity. In fact the boy's behaviour was worse than any of the other children. Cnut's daughter Freydis had stolen a sea shell, and Eric knew the good Viking girl planned to use it to free herself when the time was ripe.

Mark too noticed Olaf, and he didn't care for what he saw. But he was bound by a debt of honour to save the boy. Peter sneered at the weak boy, who had been spared of slavery.

"Mark why don't you let me talk to Francis Pen? He is the steward to the Earl of Northumberland and could get that boy castle work. Away from you, and you still have kept your word?"

"Oh I would be grateful, Peter. He is full of hate and half mad. He isn't like Einar and Gunnhild. And Gunnhild is a girl. It is sad day when a girl can beat you," Mark expressed in disgust.

Eric picked up Mark's disgust for Olaf. True the boy hadn't any of his parent's qualities but then again he had barely survived last winter. Good food and kindness could nourish his mind and spirit.

Astrid strolled passed Eric and issued a gloomy warning.

"Seasons will come and go, before that happens."

Her prediction left Eric feeling cold, of all the people in the West Settlement, Freda was his only real friend. Olaf, for all his weakness was her son. Eric prayed to Thor to cast his favor over the boy. Then Eric thought of Freda's other son, Halfdan. There was a youth more suited to live in the east with castles and churches. A flash of insight hit Eric - Thorfinn had reached Vinland. Halfdan was thriving.

"Freda I will do what I can but in the end the fight can only be won by Olaf himself, why are your sons so different?" It was a question Eric asked in the quiet of his mind.

Birds above the ship signaled to one and all land that was near.

Peter took hold of Astrid's hand.

"I descend from Einar of the Orkneys so I was told, and was told by the forest people who found me as babe, that I was wrapped in a fine woolen shawl. The woman who lay dying at my side was a nun who had been put in the Covent by her father who was a lord. No child of ours will ever go in one of those places, Astrid. I want them to learn that reading and sums, like Francis Pen can do. That is the way of the future not running around with a bow like me. But I will looking after our sheep, not going off to wars."

A dense curtain of fog draped over the ship. The Captain gulped, he was aware that many ships in sight of land had been cut by hidden rocks and the crew taken down into the sea, buried beneath the waves. The Emissary fell on his knees and prayed to St. Ann to intercede with the Lord his God, to extend mercy for the sake of their holy mission.

Peter and Eric applied their acute hearing to try and tune into the different sounds the sea was making. But Astrid's feet slid across the slippery deck and she touched the captain on the shoulder.

Her arm was stretched out as she spoke.

"St. Ann sends a message go straight ahead."

The crew crossed themselves, the Emissary rose to his feet. St. Ann had spoken through Astrid. The Captain informed the English archers.

Mark was guilty, he prided himself at being able to judge people, and he had very sadly missed out on seeing how great a prize Astrid really was.

"Peter, Astrid has the sight. This explains why St. Ann sends us to Greenland and gave you to her."

Peter was stunned. He, a lowly archer who had never done many worth deeds had been blessed by St. Ann, with wife who had the sight. He vowed to be a better man. His first born daughter would be named Ann.

"I wonder if we can train her up to detect the Scots or tax collector, Peter."

Eric was revolted by having to hear about this dead Saint. Until he looked over at Olaf and saw the boy's face glowing. Perhaps the dead hag had some uses after all. Eric went over to Olaf to encourage Olaf's new devotion.

"Trust in St. Ann she will guide you," Eric felt sick as he uttered the words.

The Emissary was so impressed by Eric's actions he broke into another sermon about God's mercy.

Astrid made signs to Peter that the sermon was about mercy. Peter made a choking sound and instantly concluded the churches in Norway produced the stupidest churchmen in entire Christendom.

Eric had to hold his breath, even annoying Halfdan couldn't excel the Emissary in voicing rubbish.

"Ah that sermon tells me much, Emissary," Grimar declared in a pious voice.

Indeed it told Grimar that he needs to take the first ship to southern Scotland. The pious prattler was sure to fire-up the Earl's wrath and stir the Earl's memories of Grimar's crime. He would kill Freydis and Olaf before he departed. He had to have some fun after enduring this voyage. It had not been very profitable for him. He had the joy of seeing his old tormentors die, but that wasn't enough. He still hadn't gained the good position in life he deserved.

The safe harbor of Kirkwood beckoned to the ship.

Astrid could scarcely hide her bewilderment; escape was in the hearts of the archers, the sailors, Grimar, and more understandably in the children. On a far distant shore Thorfinn too had yet to achieve his gaol.

But the Orkneys would astonished everyone...